# Terrifying Steamboat Stories

# Terrifying Steamboat Stories

## True Tales of Shipwreck, Death and Disaster on the Great Lakes

by James L. Donahue

New Printing by Thunder Bay Press
Holt, Michigan

Library of Congress Catalog Card Number: 90-93084

International Standard Book Number: 0-9626947-0-3

First Edition 1991
Second Edition 1995

*Dedicated to my parents, Edwin and Velma Donahue, who gave me a wonderful home at Harbor Beach, Michigan; a place where steamboats still visited during my childhood years.*

# Contents

# Part 4; Contemporary Calamities 1920 to 1975

# List of Illustrations

# Preface

This book happened when I wasn't looking. The stories came from my years of gleefully rummaging around in the fishnet-draped archives of Great Lakes history, turning out a seemingly endless number of ideas for a weekly column I wrote for the *Times Herald*, a daily newspaper published at Port Huron, Michigan.

The column was well received. Somewhere along the line I started writing stories for the *Summer Magazine*, published by the *Traverse City Record Eagle*, because folks in that part of Michigan said they liked reading about shipwrecks, too. When writing them, I never thought of the stories as material for a book. Writing for a newspaper is different, said I. There usually is much more to tell about a shipwreck than space in a daily newspaper allows, so the stories tend to be brief. There is a danger that portraits of human drama, the stuff that people really want to read about, will get lost in the facts.

Some of my friends didn't agree with me. People such as Jim and Pat Stayer, of Lexington, Michigan, divers and shipwreck research buffs, who have been faithful readers of my stories; and Jane Miller, retired director of the Sanilac County Museum in Port Sanilac, who clips the stories for a museum scrapbook every week, were among the ones who urged me to put them in a book. My wife, Doris, also said it, but though I give her credit for being a wise, talented and wonderful person, I always thought her opinion was biased.

I didn't take the idea seriously until I met Bob Mandel, publisher for the former Altwerger & Mandel Publishing Company, the people who originally produced this book. Bob also was reading my stories and urged me to develop a book about shipwrecks. We kicked around some ideas, and when the suggestion was made that we put together a collection of the best stories from my column, he liked it. When the managing editors of both newspapers gave their blessings to the project, it all came together.

Because I knew I had more freedom to expand stories for the book, a few changes were made. When possible, I added scraps of information that got clipped from the newspaper accounts, and wrote two additional stories just for this book. You can easily spot the stories especially written for this book because they are longer. They include the account of the *Eastland* disaster in Chicago, and the burning of the liner *Noronic* at Toronto.

I want to apologize to the few readers who might feel cheated because not every story in this book is about shipwreck. I tossed in a few lighter tales, such as the one about the cook who saved the steamer *Hastings* when it got turned around and went the wrong way on Lake Ontario, and the piece about the historic steamer *Argo* that made a rocky trip up the Detroit River. Think of them as comic relief.

James L. Donahue

# Introduction

Some of the older sailors still call it "steamboating," even though steam engines rarely drive the big boats on the Great Lakes anymore. Its an old phrase, lovingly clutched by men who remember how it was to work aboard a real steam powered ship. They fondly remember the feel, the sounds and even the smell of those vessels under power.

There has always been a form of romanticism about steamships. Men have been mysteriously drawn to them ever since the first awkward and very dangerous experimental vessels poked their bows into the waters of the world shortly after the start of the 19th century. The Rev. Peter Vanderlinden, a Roman Catholic priest at Port Huron, Michigan, who has entertained a lifelong hobby of photographing, collecting information about and cataloging ships on the Great Lakes, says he thinks he knows why. "Ships are the largest machines made by man. I think there is a fascination about being around them, and for some, about being able to control them," he said.

For some reason, modern vessels which are powered by diesel engines operated by buttons and levers on a control panel, have lost some of their lure. Modern sailors are well paid, well fed, and they sleep in private rooms. They share the luxury of television sets, shipboard movies, libraries and paid time off. They regard ships as giant machines. They say they don't feel drawn by the sea now. After a few years they find it easy to leave the boats and become landlubbers again.

Even though ships can still be dangerous, stories about their sinkings during savage lake storms are rare now. The *Edmund Fitzgerald,* which sank in a November gale on Lake Superior in 1975, was the last of the big ships claimed by the lakes. She probably won't be the last, but the decades that have passed since her foundering mark a welcome change. As this book will show, shipwrecks were once so frequent they were almost an everyday occurrence. Only the ones that claimed a lot of lives got much attention by the newspapers.

From the day the *Walk-In-The-Water* puffed her way across Lake Erie in 1818, until diesel engines took over, steamships dominated the Great Lakes for about 150 years. There was a time when the skyline over the lakes was black from the coal smoke of passing freighters, passenger liners, steam barges and tugboats.

At first steamboats were propelled by paddle wheels. Unlike the familiar riverboats used on the Mississippi, Great Lakes vessels carried their wheels on the side. They also were known as sidewheel steamers. The wheels could be operated independent of one another, which allowed for easy turning when one wheel moved forward while the other churned in reverse.

Propeller driven ships were introduced early in the game, and both types of propulsion were used on vessels throughout the steamboat era. The famed Detroit and Cleveland Transportation Line (D & C) of passenger ships which operated until the early 1950s were all sidewheelers. Propeller driven ships on the lakes were usually referred to as "propellers," although they also could be called "steamers." Paddle wheel driven ships were usually called steamboats, steamers or sidewheelers.

The first iron hulled steamship on the lakes was the *U.S.S. Michigan,* a government gunboat, built at Erie, Pennsylvania in 1844. The first commercial iron ship on the lakes was the *Merchant,* which went into service in 1862.

The introduction of both propellers and iron hulled ships were controversial in their day. The old timers insisted that iron ships didn't handle collisions with rocks like the wooden ships, and many insisted that paddle wheels were superior to propellers for a variety of reasons.

Steamboats burned wood at first. That was because lumber was in plentiful supply. Boats that burned wood could stop frequently along the shore to take on more fuel, a process called "wooding." The advantage was that more space aboard ship could be used to store cargo. In fact, lumber was one of the primary fuels carried by the ships for many years. The problem with wood burning ships was sparks that sometimes came out of the stacks, which in turn threatened the ship. For this reason, ships at first carried unusually tall smoke stacks.

Coal mined in New York and Pennsylvania, took the place of wood as a primary fuel aboard ships. It burned hotter, and the fires lasted longer, but the fuel had to be stored in sufficient quantity to move the ship from one end of the lakes to the other. This used up valuable cargo space on the early steamers. To compensate, the steamers usually pulled a string of barges, also loaded with cargo. The sailing ships, which were always present on the lakes, made fine barges.

The social life among sailors on steamboats was uniquely divided, both by the jobs they did and eventually the design of the ship. The engine room workers, also known as the black gang, lived at the aft end of the ship. They were called the black gang because flying coal dust at their work station blackened their skin and clothes.

The deck crew, consisting of the captain, executive officers and wheelsmen who steered the ship and determined its actions, usually lived in quarters at the bow of the vessel. They were separated from the engine room crew by the middle of the ship, where the cargo was carried. This division has disappeared on modern vessels. On many boats the bridge has been moved back to the rear of the ship and all employees live together.

The early steamers were especially dangerous. Boilers blew up. Overheated engines mounted in wooden ships sometimes started fires. Steam pipes worked loose during the stress of heavy seas, the hot steam scalding workers alive. Before there was radio and sonar, ships collided with each other and with many other things that got in their way. They hit submerged rocks and shoals. Sometimes they hit floating objects lost from decks of other ships, like logs and barrels. These objects would do bad things to wooden paddle wheels.

This book is a collection of stories about things that happened to Great Lakes steamboats, their barges and the men and women who walked their decks.

# TERRIFYING STEAMBOAT STORIES

# Part One:
# Early Horrors
# 1818 to 1879

# TERRIFYING STEAMBOAT STORIES

# The *Walk-in-the-Water*

Even though it existed only three years, the steamboat *Walk-In-The-Water* make a dramatic mark on Great Lakes history.

The *Walk-In-The-Water* was built in 1818 and was one of the pioneer steamboats of the world. It was the first steamship built on Lake Erie, the first steamship to travel on Lakes Erie, St. Clair, Huron and Michigan, and make the trip up the Detroit and St. Clair Rivers, and the first steamship to offer passenger and freight service on Lake Erie between Buffalo and Detroit. It also was the first steamship to wreck on Lake Erie.

There is a legend that the boat got its strange name from an Indian who watched Robert Fulton's famed steamship *Clermont* huff and puff its way up the Hudson River eleven years earlier. The man was amazed to see a ship moving up stream against the current without the help of sails and wind. He saw the turning paddles on the ship's side wheels and remarked that the *Clermont* "walked in the water." The builders of this new steamship at Black Rock, now part of Buffalo, New York, heard the story and used it to create a name for their vessel. The name was long and awkward to use, so people started calling the vessel "The Steamboat." It still identified *Walk-In-The-Water,* because at first, she was the only steamer operating on Lake Erie.

The *Walk-In-The-Water* was financed by a group of New York businessmen interested in starting a commercial shipping business on Lake Erie. These men included marine architect Noah Brown, who built the ship, and Robert McQueen, a machinist who designed and built the engine.

*Walk-In-The-Water* was launched in the spring of 1818 and was proclaimed an immediate success. It was an odd-looking, smoke-belching, wood-burning ship that created a sensation wherever it went. The paddle wheels looked too large for her hundred and thirty-eight-foot long hull, and the single smoke stack towered above the wooden deck. McQueen knew

3

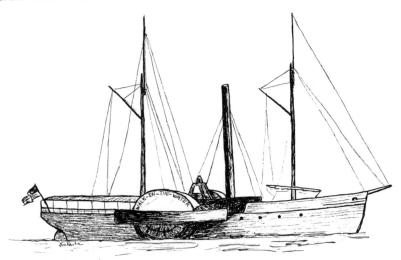

The *Walk-In-The-Water,* first steamboat on Lake Erie, as it looked anchored in Black Rock harbor, 1818.

what he was doing when he designed the stack. He didn't want embers from the wood fires under the boiler coming back down on the ship and setting it ablaze.

The boat's first trip across Lake Erie to Detroit began on August 25, with Capt. Job Fish in command. It left Buffalo with twenty-nine passengers and freight bound for Erie, Grand River, Cleveland, Sandusky and Detroit. *Walk-In-The-Water* reached Detroit in forty-four hours running time. It was said the boat's cabins were elegant and passengers considered the trip from Detroit to Buffalo as a very pleasant experience.

The *Walk-In-The-Water* made the trip into lakes Huron and Michigan during the summer of 1819 with a load of supplies for the American Fur Company at Green Bay, Wisconsin. Thus it was that she became the first steamboat to traverse the upper lakes. Strangely enough, the trip was identical to the one made by an earlier historical vessel, LaSalle's sailing ship *Griffin,* which was the first boat to enter the Great Lakes above Niagara Falls, in 1679.

There were several parallels between these two historic vessels. They were both built within a few miles of each other, in the forests of New York at the eastern end of Lake Erie. They were both built for commercial reasons. They were the first vessels of their kind to make the trip to Green Bay from the east end of Lake Erie. They both made the trip to

4

serve the fur trading industry. LaSalle bought furs and wanted to use the *Griffin* to bring them back to New York. The *Walk-In-The-Water* brought supplies to the fur business established at Green Bay. Both ships stopped at Mackinac Island while making their journeys and both ships were wrecked in storms.

The *Walk-in-the-Water* probably created more of a sensation on the lakes than the *Griffin* because the area was more heavily populated in 1818, the ship was something extraordinary that belched steam and smoke, and it survived three full seasons compared to the *Griffin's* time of a few months.

While it may have made other trips into Lake Huron and beyond, the vessel did most of its work between Black Rock and Detroit. The ship was on that route on the night of October. 31, 1821, when it got caught in the storm that wrecked it. *Walk-in-the-Water* was under command of Capt. Jedediah Rogers when it steamed out of Black Rock at about 4:00 PM, bound for Cleveland with eighteen passengers and a general cargo.

A gale developed from the southwest by 8:00 PM, when the ship was only a few miles out on the lake, and the vessel took a severe beating. The timbers creaked and groaned at every roll. Rogers found that the engines were not powerful enough to make progress against the storm, and he was fearful of turning around and trying to get back safely to Black Rock in the darkness. He ordered the anchors dropped, and tried to ride out the gale in mid-lake. One passenger, the wife of the Rev. Alanson W. Welton, said the ship anchored a few miles above the old Buffalo lighthouse. The storm got even worse that night, and after several hours of continued straining, the hull began to leak. As the gale grew in strength the anchors dragged and the vessel drifted with the wind toward the Canadian side of the lake. By 5:00 AM, Welton said the captain gave the order to cut the anchor chains so the ship could drift on the rocks at Point Albino.

Mrs. Welton's account of the wreck that morning is graphic. "Tired out with anxious watching, I had taken my berth with my children, keeping my own and their clothes on. My husband was still on deck. When the captain's summons came to the cabin passengers to turn out, as the boat was going ashore, the floor of the cabin was ankle deep with wa-

5

ter. I will not attempt to describe the anxious, prayerful, tearful upturned faces that were grouped together in the cabin of the *Walk-In-The-Water* on that terrible, cold morning as we looked into each other's faces for probably the last time."

Prayers were answered. The ship went aground near the lighthouse, and the passengers and crew were all safely removed to the lighthouse within a few hours. Before the storm was over, the hull of the *Walk-in-the-Water* was cracked and the ship declared a total wreck. The engine was salvaged and used to power the *Walk-in-the-Water's* successor, the *Superior.*

# Strange Steamer *Argo*

The first riverboat plying between Detroit and Fort Gratiot, a place located just north of Port Huron, Michigan, was the *Argo,* a very strange looking craft built by Capt. John Burtis of Amherstburg, Ontario, in 1828.

The *Argo* could probably be best described as a catamaran, although modern sailors would probably argue that point. Some might have said she was only a motorized raft. D. B. Harrington, editor of the *Port Huron Commercial,* was a passenger on the *Argo's* first trip up the Detroit and St. Clair Rivers to Fort Gratiot. He said the vessel was built on two large hollowed-out pine logs, joined together. It had a sharp bow and square stern. A deck was built on top of the logs, and a four horsepower steam engine that ran side wheels was mounted on the deck. The ship's original dimensions gave her a peculiar appearance: she was forty-two feet long but only five feet wide. Harrington said the cabin of the *Argo* was no more than canvas stretched over upright posts to serve as a windbreak.

Burtis apparently built his steamboat on the Thames River in Ontario, then brought it to Detroit and loaded cargo for a first trip up the rivers in October, 1828. The *Argo* might have been the second steamboat to visit that Michigan port. It came along only twenty-one years after Robert Fulton took his famous *Clermont* up the Hudson River at New York, and five years after the *Walk-In-The-Water* made its first trip up the rivers and into Lake Huron.

The boat attracted a lot of attention at Detroit. Many of the town's dignitaries, including Michigan Governor Lewis Cass, came to the waterfront to see the *Argo* off on her maiden trip.

Harrington described the event: "Sea stores were laid in accordingly and steam got up at eight o'clock on the morning of her departure. After considerable swaying at the hawsers, the word was given 'all aboard,' the captain ordered the lines cast off, and away she flew at the rate of about two miles an hour. Hers was a high pressure engine, and the noise made in exhausting steam resembled much the barking of a lap dog, while the smoke which issued from her chimney could scarcely have shamed an old Frenchman's pipe."

The passengers quickly discovered the *Argo* to be an "extremely cranky" craft that took an "alarming list at the least shifting of freight or passengers," another account said. At one point, the vessel struck a fishing spike jutting up from the river bottom and nearly capsized.

It took two days for the *Argo* to huff and puff her way up the river. She arrived at St. Clair around 11:00 PM the first night and tied up at Brown's wharf. The passengers were lodged at a local hotel for the night. The *Argo* arrived at Fort Gratiot the following evening at about sunset.

Burtis took the boat back to Detroit the next day and tied her up for the winter. He spent the time redesigning his craft. He expanded her width another four feet, making her more stable in the water, and built a closed-in cabin. The *Argo* made regular trips between Fort Gratiot and Detroit for the next three years.

After the steamer *General Gratiot* was put in service around 1830, the little *Argo* was retired from that run. The *General Gratiot* was a real ship that hauled more cargo and made the same trip in sixteen hours instead of two days. Passengers found the ride to be not only faster, but more comfortable.

Burtis sold the *Argo* in 1832 to L. Davenport, who used it as a ferry between Detroit and Windsor. After the vessel was scrapped, the *Argo's* engine was taken to Grindstone City, Michigan, where it served for many years at the quarries.

# *Phoenix* in Ashes

It is a paradox in Great Lakes history that one of the first major disasters involving a fire at sea happened to the propeller *Phoenix* in 1847.

The ship was named for a mythological bird of ancient Egypt that was said to have burned itself to death, then rose again fresh and young out of its ashes. This Nineteenth Century *Phoenix* burned near Sheboygan, Wisconsin, on November 21, 1847, taking an estimated two hundred and forty passengers to their deaths. Nothing ever rose from these ashes. The ship ended up a smoldering hulk that was never rebuilt.

The *Phoenix*, a two-year-old ship under command of Capt. B. G. Sweet, was heavy laden with both passengers and cargo as she pushed her way south along the Wisconsin coast that fateful day.

Nearly three hundred people, including the crew and about a hundred and fifty Dutch immigrants traveling from Buffalo to Chicago on their way west, packed the old wooden-hulled steamer. The holds were filled with general merchandise plus tons of sugar and molasses. The *Phoenix* was never designed to carry so many passengers. Only twenty five people enjoyed cabin space on the ship. The rest were crammed anywhere they could find room.

At about 4:00 AM a fireman in the engine room noticed flames on the underside of the deck over the boiler. About the same time, flames were noticed coming out of the ventilators used for moving hot air from the boiler room. Mr. House, the ship's engineer, immediately organized fire-fighting efforts among the crew members and passengers. Three pumps were manned and several water bucket lines were set up, but the fire had a good start and was soon out of control.

When the passengers realized that the ship was going to burn, panic broke out. The boat was stopped dead in the water while crew members and some willing passengers continued to work feverishly to stop the fire and save their own lives. As the fire progressed, passengers jumped into the wa-

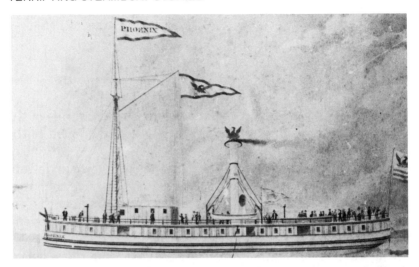

Crude drawing shows how the propeller *Phoenix* might have looked
before it burned in 1847. About two hundred forty people died.

ter. Two sisters, identified as the Misses Hazelton, of Sheboygan, joined hands and jumped overboard to drown. The
two were coming home from the east where they had been
attending school.

There were only two lifeboats and both were launched.
Captain Sweet manned one of them and the first mate got in
the other. The passengers were left to their fate. Each boat
was limited to twenty three people, which meant that most of
the people aboard the burning *Phoenix* had no way of escape
other than jumping into the water. There, even the strong
swimmers died quickly in the cold water.

Only about sixty people escaped, most of them in the
two lifeboats. The ship's clerk and engineer House lived because they climbed over the side of the ship and hung on the
rudder chains until they were rescued two hours later. The
propeller *Delaware* came on the scene while the *Phoenix* was
burning, but arrived too late to save any of the victims on her
decks. Survivors told of seeing people climb to the rigging,
then watching in horror as the fire burned the ropes and
burned all of the people clinging to them in one quick hot
flash.

Three people were pulled still alive from the water.
The porter, a brother to the mate, said he fought the fire until
the pumps quit. He jumped off the stern and swam up to the

lifeboat his brother was in. He was pulled into the boat and lived. Others who jumped into the water were not picked up, probably because the little boats were already filled beyond capacity. The *Delaware* later took all of the survivors aboard from the lifeboats.

The *Delaware* tried to tow the still-burning *Phoenix* into Sheboygan. When nearing the harbor, one of the anchors from the *Phoenix* dropped. The sailors decided to cut the chain and let the smoking hull drift up on the beach.

# Fire on the *E. K. Collins*

Canadian furniture store operator William Bartlett never expected to be a hero. Even Bartlett had to admit that he just happened to be at the right place, and have a spare boat available when one was badly needed.

The estimated seventy passengers and crew members aboard the burning steamer *E. K. Collins* needed all the help they could get on the night of Sunday, October 8, 1854. As fire engulfed the ship, destroying even the lifeboats, the people had no place to go but over the side and into the cold flowing waters of the Detroit River. Twenty-one people perished. It could have been much worse.

The handsome, two-year-old Ward Line steamer was the pride of the fleet in 1854. Built by the well-known Marine City, Michigan shipbuilder John Bushnell, the *Collins* measured two hundred fifty-nine feet in length and was lavishly furnished to draw passengers on a route that took the ship between Sault Ste. Marie and Buffalo. The boat, commanded by Capt. H. J. Jones of Detroit, was on its way to Buffalo on

Twenty-one people died when the steamer *E. K. Collins* burned on the Detroit River in 1854.

the night of the fire. It stopped briefly at Detroit to take on freight and passengers, then cast off for a night trip down the Detroit River into Lake Erie and on to Cleveland.

It was a calm night and there was an autumn nip in the air. Most of the passengers were hanging out in the ship's lounge. Many had retired to their staterooms after supper. Jones had been on the bridge all evening, piloting the *Collins* through the narrow waters of Lime-kiln Crossing, and he was starting to breath easier because the lights of Malden, Ontario, the old name for Amherstburg, were in sight. Soon the ship was expected to enter the open waters of Lake Erie.

The fire broke out somewhere on the boiler deck, just aft of the engine room, at about 8:00 PM. Some thought it might have started from a carelessly tossed ash from a smoker's pipe. The flames spread with terrible speed. An alarm was sounded, but before the crew got the hoses run out, the fire reached the engine room where the pumps were located. The engineer and fireman fled the engine room without taking time to start the pumps. Within minutes the steam was too low to keep the big paddle wheels turning and the ship became a drifting, burning death trap filled with very frightened people. All was bedlam as the fire raced through the ship's superstructure. The lifeboats burned, so nobody could use them to escape. Women screamed. People raced the fire to the bow of the ship while others leaped over the side and into the water.

Bartlett was one of several spectators on the streets of Malden who watched in horror as the burning ship floated past their town. He realized that there were people on board who needed help, and he ran to the dock where his personal boat was tied. When he arrived on the scene, Bartlett discovered fourteen people hanging on the ship's anchor chain while fire burned the deck just over their heads. He took them into his boat, then started around the burning hull, looking for others. Five more survivors were found clinging to the paddles on the port wheel, and six others were on the starboard wheel. Two swimmers were pulled from the water. Before the night was over Bartlett was responsible for rescuing twenty-seven of the forty-four people who escaped the *Collins* fire. Other survivors were picked up by the propeller *Fintry,* which pulled alongside the *Collins* so people could jump to the *Fintry's* deck.

The crew took a chance of losing their own ship to fire but Captain Langley, the *Fintry's* master, apparently felt the opportunity for saving lives outweighed the risk. Other small boats from Malden rescued still more swimmers from the water before they drowned.

The hull of the burned out ship drifted down stream until it went aground in Callam's Bay. It was towed back to Detroit where it was rebuilt as a steam barge. The boat was enrolled as a new vessel in 1857 and given a new name: *Ark*. Nine years later the *Ark* foundered with all hands during an October gale on Lake Huron.

# Mystery Wreck

In 1953 the Army Corps of Engineers removed the remains of an ancient sidewheel steamer off Fort Gratiot, Michigan, at the southern tip of Lake Huron, that had become an obstacle to the big ore carriers. The wreck caused quite a stir. When the word got out, people began searching local records to learn what vessel it was that rested so many years under their noses, in just twenty-eight feet of water.

Five big boilers and part of the shaft wheel and hub of one paddle wheel were brought up first. Then a second wheel shaft, a hand operated pump, a hatch cover, a steam cylinder, pipes of all shapes and even some oak ribs were among the relics raised. None of the pieces gave a clue as to the identity of the ship. Experts said the boilers were of a type that dated the ship before 1860. Nobody found a name stamped in the metal castings, or carved in the wood.

What they found was probably the remains of the steamer *Northerner,* which sank in that area on April 27, 1856, after a collision with the *Forest Queen.* Twelve people died in

The steamer *Northerner* was sunk in a collision with the *Forest Queen near Port Huron in 1856. Twelve people died.*

the wreck. It could have been worse. The *Northerner,* under command of Capt. Darius Cole, was steaming north from Cleveland to Saginaw with a hundred and thirty-four passengers and crew members, and about fifty tons of mixed freight. The *Forest Queen,* another sidewheeler, was bound down that night from Point aux Barques, Michigan. Her master was Captain Woodworth.

The night was dark and foggy when the two ships, lighted only by the dim glow of kerosene lamps, crossed each other's path at the wrong moment. The *Forest Queen* struck the starboard bow of the *Northerner* at about 11:00 PM, cutting the ill-fated steamer open at a point twenty feet back from the stem. She sank in six minutes.

The two vessels stuck together for about two or three of those critical minutes. Cole used the time to save as many people from his sinking ship as possible. He jumped up on the deck of the *Forest Queen* and called out, ordering everyone to climb up there with him. Cole and other crew members helped the people make the climb, which got higher and higher as the *Northerner* settled.

When the ships separated, Cole jumped back aboard his own foundering command and directed the launching of life boats so many more people escaped. Officers ran through the halls, kicking doors open and making sure everyone was awake and getting off the boat. Many of the passengers escaped in only their night clothes. The only crew member known to have died was Second Engineer Peter Moore of Cleveland. The boat's papers, including her passenger list, were lost so there was no record of the people aboard.

The fact that the *Northerner* was left forgotten in such a shallow location for so long is as much a mystery as her identity became on the day the Corps of Engineers brought her remains to the surface. Also strange: the *Port Huron Commercial,* a weekly newspaper published that year, did not mention the disaster.

It was said the *Northerner* was carrying twenty-five thousand dollars in coins and sixty kegs of whiskey in her cargo. The vessel has appeared several times in books and publications on a list of treasure finds on the Great Lakes.

The Corps of Engineers did not mention treasures

when it brought the wreck to the surface in 1953. Many of the relics were turned over to the Dossin Great Lakes Museum at Belle Isle for safe keeping.

The *Northerner* was a wooden hulled ship, built in Ohio City, the old name for Cleveland, in 1851. Captain Cole and the ship's purser, A. L. Kelsey, had just bought the vessel and were taking it on a first trip up the lake when the accident happened.

The *Forest Queen* went on to serve a colorful career as a part of the underground railroad. The boat carried former slaves, helping them escape to northern states and Canada. She foundered while under tow as a barge on Lake Erie in 1872, taking seven sailors to their deaths.

# Was the Lady Cursed?

Some said the *Lady Elgin* bore a curse from the day it was launched at Buffalo in 1851. That's because the *Lady's* engine and boilers came from the *Cleopatra,* an ocean slave trader that was confiscated by the U. S. Navy.

In spite of its dark link to the past, nobody dreamed that the *Lady Elgin* would go down in history as one of the worse disasters in Great Lakes history. When sunk in a collision on Lake Michigan, off Winnetka, Illinois, on Sept. 8, 1860, an estimated two hundred and eighty-seven passengers and crew members died.

The steamer was a monster in its day. The boat measured two hundred fifty-two feet in length and boasted over a thousand tons displacement, making it one of the largest vessels afloat on the lakes. On the day of the crash, the *Lady Elgin* was steaming north from Chicago with about three hundred excursionists, fifty ordinary passengers and a crew of thirty-five officers and men, all bound for Milwaukee. Many of the passengers were members of the Milwaukee Light Guardsmen, the German Black Jaegers and German Green Jaegers who were returning from an excursion trip to Chicago. They were preparing to join Union forces in the Civil War and were in the windy city that week to raise money for guns and equipment.

It was a night trip. The *Lady Elgin* left Chicago the night of September 7, and sailed directly into a thunderstorm. The storm brought on a full northwesterly gale by 2:00 AM. Capt. Jack Wilson wasn't worried though. He turned his ship directly into the wind and it was weathering the storm well.

Disaster came unexpectedly at 2:30 AM when the two-masted lumber schooner *Augusta* popped out of the darkness and crashed into the steamer's port side. The *Augusta,* under command of Capt. Darius Malott, was downbound with a heavy load of lumber from Port Huron, Michigan, bound for Chicago. Malott said the ship was under sail when the storm struck. The crew still was preoccupied with getting the sails

Death ship *Lady Elgin* claimed two hundred eighty-seven lives when sunk in a collision on Lake Michigan.

reefed and the ship under control when the lights of the steamer came into view just off the starboard bow.

Malott said he ordered the helm put hard about, but the ship didn't answer its rudder. Within minutes the schooner crashed into the port side of the steamer, at the midships gangway just forward of the wheel, putting a large hole in the side of the *Lady Elgin's* wooden hull. The *Augusta* pulled away from the steamer almost immediately and blew off before the wind into the night, with her foresails wrecked and her bow badly crushed and leaking.

Because of the storm, Malott said he couldn't return to the scene of the collision, but continued on to Chicago, where he reported the accident. He said he never dreamed the collision sank the steamer, which was more than twice the size of the *Augusta*.

The *Lady Elgin* was, indeed, fatally wounded. Bedlam broke out on her decks as soon as people realized the ship was sinking. The steamer was only ten miles off the Illinois coast so Wilson tried to run his crippled ship to shallow water. To gain time, he ordered the cargo and passengers moved to the starboard side. He reasoned that if he could get the ship to list in the other direction, he might get the hole in the port side raised above the waterline. Wilson also sent officers below deck with blankets, mattresses and lumber, doing all

19

they could to plug the hole that was quickly sending the elegant ship to the bottom of Lake Michigan. Nothing worked. The water eventually flooded the engine room and put out the fires. The engine crew opened the steam valves to the boilers to prevent an explosion once the cold water hit them. Then came the order to abandon ship.

The *Lady Elgin* was sinking faster than Wilson realized. Only two lifeboats were launched. It was said the boat went down about twenty minutes after it was hit. Many people ended up clinging to wreckage, mostly from the deck and upper cabins, which floated away as the ship sank under their feet.

The people were still alive, still clinging to the wreckage, when they drifted close to shore. There the high seas, still fanned by the gale, played a brutal game of death. Hundreds of people, already exhausted from hours of exposure in the water, didn't have the strength to go through this final ordeal in the surf. They either were dashed to their deaths on the rocks or drowned in the boiling waves. Bodies were stacked like cordwood on the rocky coast that day. Only ninety-eight people survived.

The disaster was so terrible that a stigma was attached to the *Augusta* from that time on. It followed the schooner everywhere it went. Her owners changed the vessel's name to the *Colonel Cook* the next year, but that didn't help. It was always remembered as the ship that sank the *Lady Elgin*. Malott died three years later when his next command, the bark *Major,* also sank in Lake Michigan. Strangely enough, it is said that the *Major* lies within ten miles of the *Lady Elgin.*

# Lost Treasure Ship

Sunken ships in the Great Lakes rarely contained treasure such as gold or jewelry. But there were exceptions. Whoever finds the sidewheeler *Keystone State* might also find a safe stocked with gold and silver coins worth millions. The money was said to have a cash value of $50,000 when the steamer sank on Saturday, November 9, 1861.

Finding this wreck will not be easy. The *Keystone State* and the thirty-three souls on her decks disappeared somewhere on Lake Huron. Historians believe the ship sank somewhere off the tip of Michigan's Thumb.

The steamer left Detroit the previous day, bound for Milwaukee with passengers and a cargo of farm tools, crates of valuable china and general merchandise. Her captain was Wilkes Traverse; the mate was Lewis Rankin. Alexander Kent was the chief engineer The *Keystone State* encountered a furious storm while still on Lake Huron and never made port. The boat was last seen rolling heavily on the seas somewhere off Point aux Barques, Michigan.

Nobody knows how this ship met its end, or where it happened. Wreckage, believed to be from the steamer, came ashore from Forestville, Michigan for fifty miles north to Point aux Barques. The wheelhouse and other debris drifted ashore near Forestville during a gale on November 19, ten days after the *Keystone State* was believed to gone down. Also that month, the steamer *Forest Queen* reported finding wreckage floating off Point aux Barques, and the upper cabins and stanchions of a sidewheel steamer washed ashore near White Rock, Michigan.

The *Keystone State* was one of the largest vessels on the lakes in its day. The ship measured about three hundred feet in length and grossed over thirteen hundred tons. She was thirty-four feet wide at the beam. One account said the ship was only two years old, built at Buffalo in 1859. Beers' *History of the Great Lakes* notes that it was an old steamer that had sailed for years between Buffalo and Chicago. Some said the *Keystone State* was in poor repair. Sailors complained that the ship was unwieldy and difficult to handle in heavy seas.

There was one other fatal flaw; the ship carried no lifeboats. When it sank, the victims on board had no way to escape. The *Keystone State* remains today one of the mystery ships of Lake Huron.

# Why Did They Hit?

The collision that sank the steamer *Pewabic* and took an estimated hundred lives in Lake Huron's Thunder Bay is still counted among the worst of the lake disasters. It also remains among the unsolved mysteries of the Great Lakes.

This accident happened when a sister ship, the *Meteor* collided with the *Pewabic,* sinking her at dusk, on the night of August 9, 1865. Nobody knows for sure why or how experienced sailors aboard the two vessels from the Lake Superior Line could have made such a mistake. The lake was calm, the night was clear, and survivors said they could see the lights of the *Meteor* coming for miles before the two boats hit.

The officers didn't have much to say about the accident. Historians have developed a plausible theory. Sailors in 1865 were hungry for news from home, and the best way for them to get it was to exchange newspapers. Ships, especially vessels affiliated with the same company, made a habit of passing newspapers to one another when they met, so sailors could get the latest news from the ports still lying ahead of them. It was said boats that passed on regular routes established a system where crew members exchanged sacks filled with newspapers and sometimes even mail when they met in mid-lake.

The *Pewabic* and the *Meteor* were on a schedule and probably passed one another regularly at about the same place on every trip. Nobody can prove it, but the story is said that the masters brought their vessels recklessly close to one another in passing so the papers could be thrown from each other's decks. The captains did not care to bring their boats to a stop and take the time to drop a yawl boat from the davits. It apparently had been done successfully before. On the night of August 9, they got too close.

The *Pewabic,* under command of Capt. George McKay, was coming down the lake, bound for Detroit, with about a hundred and seventy-five passengers and crew members, plus

About a hundred people died when a collision in 1865 sank the steamer *Pewabic* off Alpena, Michigan.

a heavy cargo including two hundred and seventy tons of copper ingots. The *Meteor,* loaded with lime, was upbound for Lake Superior

Some accounts said Capt. Thomas Wilson and the *Meteor's* first mate, George Cleveland, who was standing watch, were negligent. News stories of the period show that a jury acquitted Cleveland of any wrongdoing. Wilson testified that he was not on the bridge at the time of the crash.

When the *Meteor* drove her bow deep into the port side of the *Pewabic,* just aft of the wheelhouse, many people were crushed in the cabin where they were socializing for the evening. The *Pewabic* filled and sank so fast that crew members caught below in the engine room and passengers who failed to leave their staterooms immediately, went to the bottom with her. Some survivors escaped by jumping to the deck of the *Meteor* before she backed away. Others got in lifeboats or were picked up in the water by lifeboats launched from the *Meteor.*

Survivor James M. Buchan of Cleveland said he was standing with several other passengers on the deck, watching the approaching *Meteor,* until it became evident that the two ships were going to hit. He said everybody ran to the starboard side where they heard the crash. "It didn't shake the boat very much," Buchan said. He said he went to his state room, grabbed a life jacket, then went out on deck again to assess the damage. By then the *Pewabic* was already going down by the head. Before he knew it, Buchan said he was in the water and getting pulled down by the suction from the sinking ship. "When I began to ascend I felt pieces of timber above me and touching me all around. I began to fear that I would come under a piece of the deck and find it difficult to come to the surface. But owing to my having a life preserver in my hand, I came up more rapidly than the wreck and found myself on top of the water with a large piece of the hurricane deck under me."

The exact number of people killed was never told. Estimates ranged between forty and one hundred.

The *Pewabic* sank deep, in a hundred and eighty feet of water off Alpena, Michigan. Even there, the steamer continued to claim lives. Her cargo of copper, plus an estimated forty thousand dollars in cash from her strongbox, tempted many divers to risk the dangerous descent to the wreck. At least five divers lost their lives before salvagers successfully recovered the Pewabic's treasures in 1917.

The *Meteor* caught fire and burned about two days after the accident, even before she completed her ill-fated trip north into Lake Superior. The fire happened in the St. Marys Ship Canal Basin near Sault Ste. Marie. They said the fire was caused by the ship's leaking hull, which brought water in contact with the cargo of quick lime. To extinguish the fire, the *Meteor* was scuttled and sunk in twelve feet of water.

# Saving the Crew of the *New York*

Fifteen sailors owed their lives to the plucky crew of the Canadian schooner *Nemesis* when their ship, the propeller *New York*, was lost in a Lake Huron gale on October 15, 1876. Only one man died when the storm swamped the *New York*, sending her to the bottom off Forestville, Michigan. Fireman William Sparks, Buffalo, New York, fell overboard while trying to climb from a tossing lifeboat to the deck of the *Nemesis*. They said Sparks was exhausted from the five hours he spent in an open boat and couldn't manage the climb.

Capt. Michael Galvin was in command of the *New York* on a trip from Cove Island, on Georgian Bay, bound for Buffalo with the lumber barges *Nellie McGilura* and *R. J. Carney* and schooner *Butcher Boy* in tow, when they were caught in the storm in the middle of the lake. The four boats were holding their own until the afternoon when the tow line to the barges parted. Galvin turned his ship around and tried to toss a new line to the drifting barges, but the seas drove him off. As the *New York* turned and twisted against the rollers her wooden seams opened and the hull began taking on water.

The barges and the schooner all set sail, with the *Butcher Boy* taking the lead in the string. They ran, with their tow lines still connecting them to each other, south before the wind to Port Huron, Michigan. They made it, although the holds of both barges were filled with water and the *McGilura's* forecastle was swept away. The fact that all were wooden ships and loaded with lumber kept them afloat.

The *New York* did not fare as well. The leak got worse as the storm grew in intensity. Galvin made a run for the shore, hoping to beach the boat before it sank. The water gained until it put out the boiler fires and the ship lost power. The crew scrambled for the rigging and raised the sails, only to see the old canvas, rotted after years of storage, torn to shreds before the wind. The old propeller now was at the mercy of the storm. Immense waves constantly broke over her deck as the ship rolled wildly in the trough of the seas. Time was running out. Galvin ordered the yawl launched and the crew abandoned ship. Twenty minutes after casting off, the *New York* turned partly on her side and disappeared under the waves.

The crew spent a fearful night in the open boat, battling the wind, waves, and the cold. Snow squalls buffeted them and great seas kept everyone drenched. Constant bailing was necessary to keep the boat afloat. The sails of the *Nemesis* were sighted at dawn. The little schooner, commanded by Captain Shurse and three other sailors, spotted their boat, but it took some skillful seamanship to bring the vessel around to pick up the survivors. Handling a sailing ship in a gale is no easy task. Turning it around is nearly impossible. Many a story was told by masters of schooners in tow who helplessly watched the towing steamer founder before their eyes, and said they were unable to turn their vessel against the wind to rescue the crew.

Shurse not only did it once, he did it twelve times. He swung wide, tacking his ship carefully into the winds, which, even though diminished, were still packing a wallop. The first try at bringing the *Nemesis* alongside the bouncing little lifeboat failed, so Shurse sailed on past and turned for a second, then third, and fourth try. In the meanwhile, the seas washed away the schooner's deck load of tanbark. The loss of his cargo didn't discourage Shurse. The lives of those sixteen souls in that tossing lifeboat were more important. Perhaps he could picture himself someday in an open boat praying for someone to deliver him from the terror of the storm.

It was not until the twelfth try that the *Nemesis* succeeded in putting the little boat snugly up against the lee side of the schooner without running it down. A rope was thrown, someone caught it, and the rescue was made. The tragedy of the story was that William Sparks didn't make it. The *Nemesis* arrived in Port Huron with her human cargo of fourteen men and one woman just ahead of the barges.

The remains of the *New York* were found by Michigan sport divers in May, 1988 off Port Sanilac.

# A Dangerous Game

The captains denied it, but many said the new sidewheel steamer *Alaska* was racing with the *City of Detroit* when the steam dome on the *Alaska's* boiler exploded. Three crew members were killed and two others fatally scalded in the blast near the mouth of the Detroit River at about 10:30 AM on September 5, 1879.

About ten other crew members were hurt in the explosion which caused extensive damage to the ship. Miraculously, only two passengers were among the casualties and the vessel remained afloat. William Barning of Catawba Island was scalded in the face and hands and an unidentified woman cut her hands trying to escape from her cabin through a window.

Both ships were full of passengers and bound from Detroit to Put-In-Bay, Ohio. The *Alaska* had been stopped at Amherstburg, Ontario and taking on coal when the *City of Detroit* steamed by, its decks crowded with excursion passengers.

The *Alaska's* master, named Goldsmith, admitted that he asked his engineers, brothers John and Charles Stevens, to put on a full head of steam as the ship pulled out of the river and into Lake Erie a few hundred feet behind the other vessel. They wouldn't say it, but Goldsmith and Captain Bill McKay, skipper of the *City of Detroit,* were fond of racing one another across Lake Erie whenever the chance arose. This could well have been on his mind that autumn morning when he asked for the extra steam.

Nobody knows what happened. The boiler blew as the ship was getting up to full speed. The blast killed the Stevens brothers and fireman John Boyd. About ten other crew members working nearby were scalded. At least two of those workers later died from injuries. They were not identified. The death list might have been much higher because many people got excited and jumped in the water, either to get relief from their burns or because they were afraid of more explosions or fire. McKay brought his ship around and the *City of Detroit*

The steamer *Alaska* survived a boiler explosion on Lake Erie in 1878. Three crew members died.

was credited with saving many lives.

The U. S. Revenue Cutter *Fensenden* was in the area. She put out a tow line and brought the *Alaska* back to Detroit where the ship was taken into dry dock for repair.

The *Alaska* ended its days as an excursion steamer in 1890 when her engine was removed and the hull was converted for use as a schooner-barge. The ship was rigged as a propeller barge in 1895 and worked in the Canadian lumber trade for another fifteen years before it was destroyed by fire at Tobermoray, Ontario, in 1910.

# The Cook Who Commandeered Her Ship

In the old days women never played leadership roles on Great Lakes ships. They were present on the boats and once in a while they proved their ability to compete with the best of the sailors.

Such was the case of Martha Hart, cook on the steamer *Hastings,* who in 1878 brought her ship and passengers safely home to Oswego, New York, after the officers abandoned the bridge and the wheelsman lost his bearings during an Independence Day trip across Lake Ontario.

The *Hastings* was making regular trips that summer between Oswego and Kingston, Ontario, and business apparently was good. The ship left Oswego that morning with from three to four hundred passengers for a six-hour excursion across the lake. It was due back at 9:00 PM. Hart said the *Hastings* left Kingston at 5:30 PM. For some unexplained reason, the officers left the bridge that night and a wheelsman was left in command of the ship. "No captain or mate was giving any orders," she said.

The ship was apparently wandering for a while because Hart started to notice something was wrong when they didn't make Oswego's dock by the scheduled time. She went to the bridge to investigate at about 11:00 PM, after she felt the boat make a ninety degree turn in the lake.

Hart, a twelve-year veteran sailor, found the wheelsman alone in the pilot house. She also learned, to her horror, that the man had mistaken a light from the passing steamer *City of Toledo,* bound for Kingston, to be the Oswego light, and was following the steamer north toward the Duck Islands. She said she tried to convince him that he was going in the wrong direction. She spotted the real Oswego light. "I pointed it out, but the wheelsman thought he knew better and refused to steer for it," she said.

When the *Hastings* was getting dangerously close to the islands, Hart said she went to the engine room and explained the situation to the chief engineer. He believed her

Steamer *Hastings,* shown as the *Eurydice,* was brought safely into Oswego harbor by the cook during an incident in 1879.

and stopped the engines, setting the ship adrift with several hundred alarmed passengers aboard.

Since the *Hastings* was designed as a short excursion boat, there were no staterooms or beds aboard. Thus everyone spent an uncomfortable night. Fortunately the night was clear and the lake was smooth. The ship drifted until the North Star appeared at about 2:30 AM. Once she saw it and got her bearings, Hart took charge of the bridge. "I told them they were near Sackett's Harbor, below the Galloup, and told them to point south, and pointed out the direction to Oswego," she said.

Hart apparently enjoyed her brief role in command of the ship. She told how she abandoned the kitchen and remained on the bridge until the *Hastings* arrived in Oswego at 7 AM. She said she used some marine glasses that she borrowed to help her spot important landmarks.

"I told the passengers if they set the table to go for it. They didn't set any table and we didn't have a bite to eat."

The newspapers said the incident excited "both ridicule and indignation," but nobody explained what happened to the captain or officers during the trip. In fact, they were never named.

# Part Two:
# Mass Hysteria
# 1880 to 1899

# Raising the *City of St. Catherines*

When you think of the primitive equipment they worked with, divers and salvagers did amazing things before the turn of the century. Few salvage operations, however, were as spectacular as the raising of the propeller *City of St. Catherines,* a Canadian vessel sunk in a collision off White Rock, Michigan, on July 12, 1880.

The *St. Catherines,* under command of a Captain McMaugh, was making a fast trip from Montreal, Quebec, to Chicago with passengers and freight when it collided with a downbound steam barge, the *George H. Morse,* at 2:30 AM.

Each crew blamed the other. Captain Hart, master of the *Morse,* said the night was clear and the ships were both well lighted and clearly visible as they approached one another. He said the wheelsman on the *City of St. Catherines* unexpectedly turned the ship to port and ran it across the bow of the *Morse.* The first officer of the *St. Catherines* had a different story. He charged that the wheelsman on the *Morse* unexpectedly turned that ship hard to starboard as the two vessels approached, and caused the crash. The *Morse* struck the *St. Catherines* near the forward gangway on the port side, driving its bow deep into the liner's wooden hull. The crash shoved in the *St. Catherine's* side "as if it had been an egg shell," he said. The ship sank in fifteen minutes.

Many of the people on the *St. Catherines* scrambled aboard the *Morse* during the few minutes the two vessels were driven hard against each other. Others launched lifeboats and some people jumped in the water. The propeller *David W. Rust* came on the scene with schooners *D. K. Clint* and *I. C. Butts* in tow. The three vessels stopped to participate in rescue work.

Hart said he feared the *Morse* was sinking, so he transferred passengers and crew members that had boarded his boat from the *St. Catherines* to the *Rust.* The *Rust* towed the *Morse* into Port Huron. The *City of St. Catherines* sank in ninety feet of water. Her cabins and wheelhouse floated off

*City of St. Catherines* was salvaged two years after it sank from a collision in ninety feet of water in Lake Huron.

and washed ashore near White Rock. The cargo, which included hundreds of cases of choice wines and liquors, prompted several salvage efforts. Divers worked most of the summer of 1882, trying to raise the hull. The job involved getting heavy cable or chains under the hull and then attaching them to giant ballast tanks.

Weeks passed, and there was much speculation that the project would fail. Then in September, just before bad weather set in, the salvagers pumped air into the ballast tanks and raised the hull a few feet from the bottom. Tugs pulled the wreck, still submerged and partly buoyed up by the tanks, north into Harbor Beach harbor. There, under protection of the big breakwalls, the steamer was finally raised, temporary repairs made to the hull, and the water pumped out.

The *St. Catherines* was towed to Detroit where it went into dry dock. It was rebuilt and refitted there for commercial lake trade as the propeller *Otego,* which made its first trip in May 1883 to Bay City as a lumber barge.

# Burning of the *Marine City*

When the *Marine City* went up in smoke off Lake Huron's Sturgeon Point on August 28, 1880, the fire came close to being a major marine disaster. As it was, eight people of the estimated hundred and fifty-five passengers and crew members perished. That the others survived was considered a miracle.

Capt. William E. Comer was taking the ship on a routine trip up the lake, stopping at various ports between Port Huron and Mackinaw City. The fourteen-year-old wooden hulled ship was carrying about a hundred and twenty passengers, many from Port Huron, Detroit, and Ohio ports. The ship also was loaded with general cargo, including thirteen hundred pine and cedar railroad ties, fifty thousand shingles in the forward and aft holds, and twenty cords of cedar posts piled on the main deck.

Passenger E. L. Stephenson of Cincinnati said he and three crew members were swapping stories on the main deck when the fire broke out in a fuel bunker under the deck. The crew rolled out fire hoses but when they tried to charge the lines, they discovered the water valves were rusted shut. The fire was spreading rapidly and Stephenson thought the passengers should be warned. The first mate, however, told everyone to keep quiet because he didn't want to stir a panic. The word got out anyway. A cook noticed the fire and before he could be stopped, ran through the ship yelling "fire" at the top of his voice. The mate was quite right; bedlam broke out.

In the meantime, Captain Comer was in his cabin and wasn't told about the fire right away either. Once he knew, however, Comer took charge and was credited with saving many lives. People said he acted with a cool self-assurance that calmed many of the passengers and helped them escape alive.

Comer first ordered the *Marine City* turned and run at full speed toward shore, which was about two miles away. As the fire swept through the engine room the black gang fled for their lives. Before he left the engine room, the chief engineer shut off power to the wheels so everybody would have a chance to escape by launching the ship's life boats. That decision, Comer's leadership, and the fact that the tugboat *Vulcan* was nearby and able to draw alongside the burning steamer to take people off before the fire reached them, helped avert a major tragedy. The Sturgeon Point lifesaving station saw the fire and lifesavers managed to get a boat to the scene in time to pull other survivors from the water. Two other ships, the steamer *Metropolis* and tug *Grayling,* also helped.

The eight who died were said to have drowned because they lost their nerve and jumped overboard. The dead included Frank Emmett of Port Huron, Martin T. Watson, a Detroit businessman, crew members Richard Schultz and James Cook, passengers James Graffin and Guy McElroy, both of Toledo, and a Dr. Pomeroy, also of Ohio.

Comer, and a passenger, Mrs. A. B. Clough, both received recognition for their bravery. Crew members presented Comer with a gold watch. Clough got a silver tea set from the parents of Joseph Voight, a six-year-old Detroit boy who she found wandering lost on the burning ship and put safely aboard a lifeboat.

**Eight people died when the steamer *Marine City* burned off Lake Huron's Sturgeon Point in 1880.**

# Duncan and Christy

The wreck of the steamer *Asia* in Lake Huron's Georgian Bay on September 14, 1882 had all of the elements of a Hollywood production; terror, drama at sea, a captain who displayed wanton disregard for human life, and even the possibility of romance.

There were only two survivors out of the hundred and twenty-five passengers and crew members. They were seventeen-year-old Duncan A. Tinkis and eighteen-year-old Christy Ann Morrison, who stumbled ashore in a remote wilderness in Ontario, Canada, after spending a fearsome night in an open boat. An Indian found them and brought them by canoe to Parry Sound two days later. A ballad was written about the wreck of the *Asia* and sung by the natives around Owen Sound for many years.

The foundering of the *Asia* is still counted among the worst disasters in Great Lakes history. Some said the wreck was caused by carelessness on the part of the *Asia's* master, Capt. John Savage. Had Savage lived, Canadian authorities might have found him guilty of taking the boat out of port after the vessel was denied a license because it did not contain enough life jackets and life boats to handle even a maximum-size crew. He also overloaded the *Asia* with ninety-seven passengers when the ship was designed to carry forty. There was one other serious problem. The *Asia* was a flat-bottomed vessel, originally built for river duty, and veteran sailors said she was not able to handle the rigors of a storm on the open waters of Georgian Bay.

The *Asia* was not only laden with passengers when she steamed out of Owen Sound around midnight on September 13, she also was loaded to the gunwales with heavy machinery, horses and supplies bound for a logging camp at French River. No one knows why Savage took his ship out of port while a gale was already pounding the lakes into a frenzy. Authorities later censured Savage "for want of judgment in leaving the port in the face of a storm."

Tinkis and Morrison told about their experience. They said it was a terrible night for the passengers, all of them crammed in whatever shelter they could find. Some of them were trying to sleep on chairs, while others were sprawled on the pitching deck. As top heavy as she was, the *Asia* pitched and turned like a wild animal as the storm intensified. Many people were seasick. "Dishes and chairs were flying in every direction," said Tinkis, who was traveling with his uncle, J. H. Tinkis.

By morning, Savage knew his boat was in trouble. Waves were thundering over her decks and the ship was taking on water. Morrison said she heard the men pitching cargo and even the horses over the railings just outside her stateroom at about 11:00 AM. She said she looked out, saw her cousin, First Mate John McDonald, and asked him what was going on. McDonald had a look of despair on his face as he told her they were "doing all we can do." Not long after that the *Asia* foundered. Morrison said she put on a life jacket and waited in her room until the ship tilted over and water began coming in under the door. Then she climbed out on the deck and held a railing. "The boat seemed to be settling down. I saw a lifeboat nearby and lowered myself into the water. The captain caught me and held me from sinking until the mate (McDonald) came and helped me into the boat."

Tinkis said that when he and his uncle decided to leave their cabin, "the boat was rolling so badly we had difficulty getting up on the deck. I got a life preserver and put it on. The boat went into a trough of the sea and would not obey her helm. She rolled heavily for about twenty minutes and then was struck by a heavy sea. She went down with her engines running at about half past eleven."

He said he thought three lifeboats got away. "I was in the first boat. About eight others were with me at first, but more got in until the boat was overloaded and turned over twice." Tinkis said the water was filled with struggling people who were grabbing at anything to stay afloat. After being tossed from the lifeboat, he said he found himself in great danger because people began grabbing him and his life preserver. To get away from them, he said he pealed off the life preserver and swam away. "People were hanging on the spars and other parts of the wreckage. I swam to the captain's boat,

40

The *Asia* killed one hundred and twenty-three people when it sank in a gale on Georgian Bay.

which was nearby, and asked Mr. John McDougall, the purser, to help me in. He said it was of little use, but gave me his hand." There were eighteen people in the boat, including Miss Morrison, when he first got aboard. Shortly after that, the high waves tipped the craft. When the boat righted itself, Tinkis said several people were missing, including the morose McDougall.

Tinkis and Morrison said the boat tipped two more times that afternoon, each time spilling more people into the cold and frothing sea. By evening, only seven survivors remained, including Captain Savage and McDonald. Morrison said she discovered that by wrapping her arms around the lifeline attached to the gunwales of the lifeboat, she could stay with the craft each time it rolled over. She said she just held on "so when she righted I was in again."

Everyone was wet and cold and suffering from exposure. "Our boat was full of water and the sea was constantly rolling over us," Tinkis said. "One of the first to die was the cabin boy. A wave washed him overboard. The next to go was a deck hand. He was near the gunwale and jumped out. I could see him paddling around in the water. Morrison said nobody talked all the time they were together in the open boat. After the sun went down they noticed the light from the

41

lighthouse at Bying Inlet and it seemed to cheer everybody up, knowing that land was close. "We sang a couple of sacred songs," she said.

McDonald died around midnight, and Savage died about ten minutes later. Tinkis said Savage was the last to die. He said he was holding the captain in his arms when it happened. Before morning, all of the men in the boat were dead. Only Morrison and Tinkis remained alive.

The boat drifted ashore near Pointe Au Barrie around daylight. The area was barren, with no sign of civilization, except an oil-well derrick spotted a few miles down the coast. "I put the bodies out on the beach and pried the boat off with an oar, but I could not bale it out," Tinkis said. "Miss Morrison and I went down the beach in the boat to the derrick." There they huddled together, cold, wet and frightened for still another night. The Indian discovered them there the next day and brought them out of the wilderness.

In case you wonder, Morrison and Tinkis did not fall in love and get married. They went their separate ways after that.

# Crash at the Lumber Pile

A large lumber pile at the mouth of the Black River was blamed for a collision that sank the ferry steamer *Grace Dormer* at Port Huron on July 25, 1883.

Capt. Ed Thomas, master of the seventy-six-foot-long ferry, was criticized for driving the boat blindly out of the Black River and into the busy St. Clair River without blowing the whistle. But Thomas also was praised for daring action which saved the passengers on the *Grace Dormer.*

The accident happened at about 1:00 PM as the *Dormer* was pulling out of Port Huron with about thirty passengers, bound for Sarnia, Ontario, just across the river. As the ferry cleared the Black River, Thomas was shocked to see the tug *Frank Moffatt* appear from the other side of the wood pile. The two boats were only a hundred feet apart and the *Moffatt,* operated by Capt. William O'Neill, was on a collision course.

"I put the wheel hard to starboard to turn downstream and blew the whistle three times," Thomas said. "But the tug came right on, not altering her course a hair."

The *Moffatt's* bow hit the port side of the *Dormer,* cracking the ferry's wooden hull. Before the two ships pulled away, Thomas said many of the passengers and some of the *Dormer's* crew jumped to the deck of the tug because it was obvious that the ferry was going to sink.

"When the boats separated, I found my engineer aboard the tug. I rushed to the engine and gave her a full head of steam, then ran back to the wheel and headed for the Black River," Thomas said.

It was a race against time. As the steamer moved up the river it settled deeper and deeper in the water. "Passengers were grabbing life preservers and getting ready to swim as I swing her up alongside McMorran's Dock. It wasn't necessary to throw out a gang plank or offer assistance to help anybody off. They were on the dock as soon as I was."

The ferry *Grace Dormer* docked at Port Huron, Michigan. The boat was sunk in a collision on the Black River in 1883.

In about two minutes the *Dormer* touched bottom in thirteen feet of water. The ferry was raised and repaired. The *Dormer* operated on the lakes until a fire claimed her in 1925.

# Sinking of the East Saginaw

It was for the lack of a tugboat that the steam barge *East Saginaw* was lost on Lake Huron. The trouble started at about 10:30 PM on September 25, 1883 when the steamer, with four barges in tow, drove up on Craine's Point, about a mile south of the Harbor Beach breakwater.

Captain Harry Richardson said the boat was battling a northwesterly gale and trying to make the harbor when it hit the rocks. The crash broke the ship's rudder and the subsequent pounding put holes in the wooden hull.

Richardson sent the first mate and two other sailors ashore in a yawl to get help. The plan was to get a tug to pull the *East Saginaw* off the reef and bring it into port. The tug *Adams* got up steam and went out to take a look, but the skipper said he was afraid to get too close in the storm because he didn't want to put his own vessel on the reef. He turned the *Adams* around and put back into the harbor.

In the meantime, the crew was working frantically to save the *East Saginaw*. While the barges remained anchored offshore, waiting out the night's drama, the steamer's crew hoisted sail and let the strong offshore winds work the ship off the rocks and into deeper water. The hull pulled free at about 2:00 AM, but without a rudder and with the engine room flooded, she was a helpless derelict on the stormy lake. The winds blew the drifting boat southeast and away from shore.

Richardson said he didn't realize there wasn't going to be a tug available that night. He didn't even bother to drop anchor because he expected help to arrive at any moment. Richardson set the fourteen crew members to work pumping and bailing; trying to keep the ship afloat until the tug arrived. One unidentified sailor said: "everybody bailed with might and main, while the captain kept a lookout for a tug from the pilot house. The yawl boat was made ready and was hanging from the davits so that no time would be lost if it came to the worst. From about 2:00 AM, when the steam barge got off the point until about 7:00 AM we kept it afloat. At seven

45

o'clock the water was up level with the deck and all hope was abandoned. It was about eight miles from land, having drifted in the night."

That was when Richardson gave the order to abandon ship. The men got in the little boat and kept on the lee side of the *East Saginaw* and out of the gale until the end. They said the ship remained upright as it sank. As it slipped under the water, a large black cloud of smoke burped from the stack. Then it was over. After that, the men struggled just to keep the yawl boat headed into the gale and baled out. They were still battling the storm a few hours later when the propeller *Conemaugh* stopped to pick them up.

During the rescue the yawl struck the ship's propeller guard and capsized, tossing seaman William Eccles Jr. into the water. There were some anxious moments, but Eccles was saved.

The *East Saginaw* lies somewhere off White Rock, southeast of Harbor Beach.

# "She Will Be My Coffin"

Capt. John McKay had a love for the sea and an equal love for his fellow man. He had the best of both worlds. As an experienced master, he commanded some well known steamboats on the Great Lakes in the 1870s, including the *Dubuque, St. Paul* and *Norman*. His position put him in contact with many people, both passengers and businessmen, among the port towns of Lake Superior. The *Cleveland Herald* once said he was so well loved and respected that a coastal town on "the north side of Lake Superior" once bore his name: McKay's Harbor.

Even though his last command, the twelve-year-old steamer *Manistee* was not so accommodating as some of the newer steamboats in 1883, people liked to book passage on it because they said they preferred traveling with "Johnny McKay." They were drawn to the man because McKay loved people. It was said that he carried that devotion to his death when the *Manistee* foundered in a bad Lake Superior storm off Bayfield, Wisconsin on November 16, 1883.

Stories and letters of tribute to Captain McKay appeared in newspapers from Duluth to Buffalo. Although there were no known survivors, one enterprising reporter for the *Cleveland Herald* wrote on December 8 that three people made it to shore in an open life boat after suffering a perilous time on Lake Superior.

One of these survivors, who remained unidentified, told a wonderful story about how McKay refused to leave his sinking ship because nearly all the life boats were smashed or carried away by the storm. It was obvious that somebody must be left behind. "I am captain of this boat, and if she is a coffin for anybody, she will be my coffin," he was quoted as saying. The quote turned the well-liked Captain McKay into a somewhat heroic figure, but there is no proof that he ever said it.

The record shows that the *Manistee* was swallowed up by Lake Superior with all twenty-three souls who were aboard the ill-fated ship. There were no survivors. Most of the people

Capt. John McKay died with twenty-two other people when the steamer *Manistee* sank on Lake Superior

who died were crew members but there were a few passengers.

McKay was bringing his command from Duluth, Minnesota, to Ontonagon, Michigan, with a load of flour, oats and other merchandise. The *Manistee* called at Bayfield, Wisconsin, and laid over for three days because of bad weather. Some of the passengers transferred to the steamer *City of Duluth* at Bayfield because the *Duluth* planned to go directly to Houghton, which apparently was their destination.

When the three-day storm appeared to be ending the evening of November 15, the *Manistee, City of Duluth,* and a third steamer, the *China,* all left Bayfield within a few hours of each other. The *Manistee* was never seen again. The tug *Mayhem* found a wooden bucket and a piece of the ship's pilot house about forty-five miles northeast of Ontonagon about a week later. For months after that, pieces of wreckage, including barrels of flower and furniture, washed ashore on the Keweenaw Peninsula.

The cause of the disaster remains one of the great mysteries of Lake Superior. Records show that the storm continued to abate that night although the seas were still high and conditions for sailing were not the best. Both the *City of Duluth* and *China* sailed after the *Manistee* left Bayfield and these vessels were running directly behind the *Manistee*. Left unexplained is why the ship sank, why the trailing boats failed to notice it was in trouble, and why the crew failed to escape in the steamer's life boats. No bodies were found. It was almost as if the boat had dropped through a crack.

# Wreck of the Oconto

First mate Charles Rearden of Port Huron told a story of stark terror at sea when his ship, the steamer *Oconto*, got caught in a thundering northeastern gale and blinding snowstorm the night of December 4, 1885.

The hundred forty-three-foot vessel, under command of Capt. G. W. McGregor of Lexington, left Oscoda at 4:00 PM and was steaming north along the Michigan shore for Alpena. The *Oconto* was carrying forty-seven passengers and crew members, a hundred tons of freight, plus an unknown number of cows and horses. The upper decks were packed with cutters and sleighs, plus crates filled with about a hundred chickens and turkeys. That overloaded old wooden boat was not prepared for the winter blast that awaited her on Lake Huron. What began as a three-hour, seventy-mile long trip up the lake shore quickly turned into a two-day experience in endurance.

As the storm developed and the seas began sweeping the decks, Captain McGregor decided not to try to make Alpena. Instead, he turned the ship around, aiming for Tawas Bay. A heavy wet snow began falling, and before long the *Oconto* was running blind, Rearden said. The ship was rolling violently and all was chaos below deck. "After supper the horses and cattle broke loose. The cattle were thrown in all directions. A gangway was broken in and stanchions were broken. I saw that one cow had a broken leg," he said.

While the men were struggling with the livestock, Rearden said he heard William Brown, the ship's cook, yelling for help. He later found Brown dead in his bed, apparently from fright, and the galley stove was glowing red hot. Fearing a fire aboard ship, Rearden dowsed the fire in the stove.

As great seas swept the decks, the chickens, turkeys and sleighs were all swept overboard. Up on the bridge, Captain McGregor was using all of his skill to try to bring his ship safely through the gale. As darkness closed in, McGregor

The *Oconto* gave forty-seven people a wild wintry ride on Lake Huron's Saginaw Bay. The cook died of freight.

began getting glimpses of a light ahead and steered for it. What he saw turned out to be the lighthouse on Charity Island. McGregor guessed where he was and ordered a new course just moments before the *Oconto* hit the rocks, Rearden said. "We struck a couple of times and then checked down. After that we put on all steam and let her go on the beach as far as she would go," he said.

Everybody stayed aboard the wreck for two days before the storm abated enough for a lifeboat to safely reach the island. They spent another night at the lighthouse until a ship took them back to the mainland.

The *Oconto* was salvaged the next spring. After going through extensive repair, the boat made one final voyage through the lakes to New York. On July 6, 1886, it struck a shoal on the St. Lawrence River, put a hole in its bottom, and then sank in a hundred ninety-two feet of water.

# The Ship That Wouldn't Turn Left

The collision was so violent it knocked seaman Dennis Harrington from the deck to his death in fog-shrouded Lake Michigan. It happened somewhere in the middle of the lake on the night of July 8, 1886. The steambarge *C. Hickox,* lumber-laden and bound from Muskegon to Chicago, drove her bow deep into the port side of the steamer *Milwaukee,* which was traveling empty.

The hole in the *Milwaukee's* side sank the ship, but not before the *C. Hickox* took off the rest of the crew.

Both masters, Capt. "Black Bill" Alexander of the *Milwaukee,* and Simon O'Day of the *Hickox,* had their licenses temporarily revoked after U. S. Steamboat Inspectors decided they shared the blame due to carelessness. But sailors who served aboard the eighteen-year-old wooden hulled *Milwaukee* said they thought a peculiar quirk of their ship, and Alexander's long familiarity with that quirk, may have contributed the most to the collision.

They said the *Milwaukee's* hull had warped over the years, and her starboard quarter had fallen several inches. It hung down in the water even when the ship was in light trim. Alexander always said he preferred to turn to starboard because the ship responded better to a starboard rudder than it did to port. Thus it was, when watchmen spotted the lights of the *C. Hickox* dead ahead in the fog, Alexander ordered the ship turned to starboard when the command should have been to port. O'Day ordered his ship turned to port at about the same time, which kept the vessels on a collision course.

The *C. Hickox* hit the *Milwaukee* so hard amidships that the empty steamer almost turned turtle. Sailors said it tipped on its port side at an extreme angle before settling back on her keel. It was at that moment that Harrington was apparently knocked off the deck to drown unnoticed by the others. There was mass bedlam for a few minutes aboard the *Milwaukee,* but they said Alexander restored order with a cool hand that left quite an impression.

Some people said Capt. "Black Bill" Alexander caused the collision that sank the *Milwaukee* because he ordered the ship turned in the wrong direction.

Because the *Hickox* already was backed away and lost in the fog, Alexander put the crew to work at the pumps, trying to keep the stricken ship afloat as long as possible until help arrived. He knew from the damage that the ship was going down. He used the steam left in the boilers to sound the ship's whistle, over and over again, until O'Day traced the noise and found the sinking ship once again in the fog. O'Day said: "I worked the boat carefully in the direction from which they (the whistles) seemed to come from, but, strange to say, fully three-quarters of an hour elapsed before I sighted her masthead light."

At about the same time the *Hickox* pulled alongside, the *City of New York* also arrived at the scene. After the *Hickox* took the crew aboard, the *City of New York* tried to take the *Milwaukee* in tow. It was too late. The Milwaukee settled so rapidly that the tow line had to be cut. The ship sank by the stern.

# The Ship that Burned East Tawas

The steamer *Sea Gull* caused one of the worst fires in the history of East Tawas, Michigan. It happened on July 5, 1890, when East Tawas was a major lumber port.

The *Sea Gull* was in the harbor that day to take on a cargo of ice from the Youngstown Ice Company, and was scheduled to leave for Cleveland. Her departure was delayed when a northeasterner blew up in the afternoon. The captain moored the ship at the nearby Sibley and Bearinger Lumber Company dock, which offered it shelter from the gale.

The origin of the fire was never known. Some suggested arson, but it was never proven. Flames were discovered roaring through the wooden-hulled ship at about midnight and the crew barely had time to scramble to safety from their bunks. The cook, Maggie Comett, didn't make it. She perished in her quarters.

Before local fire fighters arrived, the flames, fanned by stiff offshore winds, spread to the dock and the high stacks of lumber stored there. Firefighters from the village, lumbermen and area tug boats were soon on the scene, battling a major fire that was not only destroying the *Sea Gull,* but sweeping the Sibley and Bearinger Lumber Company.

It was common in those days to cut the lines of a burning ship so the fire wouldn't spread to the dock. In this case, the *Sea Gull's* lines were cut after the dock was already afire. They might have burned loose. If it was deliberate, the cutting of this ship's lines was not a very wise thing to have done. The burning *Sea Gull* floated off into the harbor, blown by the winds to spread the fire wherever she went.

The fire ship first bumped into the anchored steamer *Calvin,* setting that vessel on fire. Then it drifted down the shore. People from nearby Tawas City watched the flames break out in place-after-place along the harbor front as the ship was moved by wind and current along its destructive course. Several other stacks of lumber were torched. A local newspaper said the display was spectacular to watch. "No fireworks of human design could equal the display produced by the roaring mass of lumber," the writer said.

For a while the fire threatened to spread through the village. Lumber crews used dynamite to cut off the flames and save the town. Before its work was done, the *Sea Gull* spread fire for about a mile along the harbor, igniting an estimated sixteen million board feet of prime Michigan pine and hardwood.

Burned that night were the property of four lumber companies, their docks and lumber stacks, an ice house tram, and two ships. The lost lumber alone was estimated at over three hundred thousand dollars, which was big money in 1890.

# Mystery Blast at Chicago

It began as a typical summer night at the Chicago docks, July 10, 1890. The crack Union steamship *Tioga* was in port, her engines still burping excess steam from a fast run from Buffalo, and the stevedores were hard at work removing cargo from her holds.

As many as sixty men may have been aboard that night, many of them there to unload a wealth of cargo consisting of general merchandise and barrels of petroleum products. There had been a change of shift. The daytime stevedores who received hourly wages had gone home. The night crew, all on monthly salaries and all Negroes, were now on the job. The men were stripped to the waist as they hoisted the heavy containers from the belly of the iron ship.

As darkness began to build, the ship's porter, William Palmer, lit kerosene lanterns so the unloading could continue through the night. Palmer left the hold and was in another part of the ship when the stern was wracked by a terrible explosion and flash fire at 7:32 PM. An estimated twenty-seven men died and many others were badly hurt. The blast was so powerful it knocked other workers in the forward hold and on the nearby dock off their feet. Witnesses said the wooden deck of the ship was lifted. The explosion also caused extensive damage to the nearby dock and shattered windows in buildings on both sides of the river.

Strangely enough, the cause of the explosion and a second blast that left two workers seriously burned the next day was never explained. The most commonly accepted story was that fumes from some of the barrels of oil were ignited when workers brought kerosene lamps into the hold at dusk. L. Scott, a workman who survived, said he left the hold to get some air just minutes before the explosion because the smell of kerosene was choking him. "The air was very strong," he said. Capt. Austin A. Phelps wouldn't accept that story. "We had no gasoline or naphtha aboard. We did have a hundred barrels of crude petroleum in there, but that would not have

A mysterious explosion ripped the crack steamer *Tioga* at Chicago in 1890, killing about twenty-seven workers.

exploded. The remainder of the cargo was general merchandise, of which only the rear deck load had been taken off."

Phelps said the boiler didn't explode and he quickly put an end to a rumor that the ship might have been sabotaged by two former sailors who had been put ashore at Buffalo. "Two of my men were taken sick in Buffalo. I had to ship two new men in their stead. Aside from these two men, I have had all my men for several years. My crew was composed of twenty-five men, only two of whom were killed."

The dead sailors were identified as lookout E. Levally and watchman William Cuthburn, both of Buffalo. Second engineer George Haige, also of Buffalo, was so badly injured he died a few days later in a Chicago hospital. Among the others killed were Frank Burns, a steamfitter who went aboard to visit the engineer moments before the explosion, and John Neill, stevedore foreman, who was the only man who knew the number of people at work on the *Tioga* when the blast occurred. Neill's death made it almost impossible for workers to get an accurate count or identification of the dead. Some bodies were blown away from the ship and into the river. Harbor tugs and Chicago fire fighters were at the scene minutes after the blast. It was said at least fifty different streams of water were trained on the burning ship. When the fire was out two hours later, the *Tioga's* stern was resting on the bottom of the river. The gruesome job of recovering bodies was delayed until the hull was pumped out.

The pumps were still running the following afternoon when workers from the wrecking crew, Hans Christiansen and Thomas Johnson went into the hold with a lantern to work on a clogged suction pipe. Their lantern apparently caused a second explosion that rocked the ship. Both men were pulled out of the hold alive, but seriously burned and bruised.

Even though she was badly damaged, the *Tioga* was rebuilt and served the lakes for many years. The boat ended her days when she stranded off Eagle River on Lake Superior during a November storm in 1919.

# Runaway Fireship

After twenty-one years the wooden-hulled propeller *Annie Young* was considered an old vessel when she caught fire and burned off Lexington on a breezy October day in 1890. Before the day was over, nine crew members died, the *Annie Young* was a blackened hulk at the bottom of Lake Huron, and the skipper of a rescue ship, the *Edward Smith,* was in line for a medal.

No one would have guessed her black fate the day the *Young* steamed away from J. W. Thompson's dock at Port Huron for her final journey north into Lake Huron. It was sometime around 7:00 AM on October 20 that Capt. Hugh Miller ordered the ship's lines cast off and the coal fires stoked for the trip north to some of the many ports along the Michigan shoreline. The holds were loaded with a cargo of coal, barrels of nails and several hundred barrels of oil. There was a brisk northwest wind blowing, so Miller called for extra steam. He knew he needed the power to help the one hundred eighty-seven-foot vessel the moment it left the protection of the St. Clair River and put its prow deep into a line of heavy seas rolling across the length of the lake.

The steamer *Edward Smith,* with two barges in tow, also was entering Lake Huron at about the same time that morning. The *Young* had no tow so was making good time. She pulled ahead of the *Smith* and soon only the smoke from the trailing steamer's stack could be seen against the sky.

The fire broke out in the after hold at about 9:00 AM, when the *Young* was off Lakeport, Michigan. Nobody knew the cause. A fire at sea is always a fearsome thing, but it was especially terrifying for the twenty-three members of the *Annie Young's* crew. Their vessel was a wooden ship, filled with highly flammable coal and barrels of oil. It was the wrong cargo to be carrying when battling a fire aboard ship. The stories of what happened that day are filled with drama at sea. There was heroism, terror, and perhaps even a hint of insubordination. From the moment the fire was discovered,

59

the chief engineer and members of the engine room crew did all they could to put the fire out. They had two hoses hooked up to the steam pumps. It was a hard fight and some of the men suffered burns. The fire gained and it was not long before the engineer and his fire crew were driven from the after hold by the flames. At about the same time workers were driven from the engine room in great haste. They left without shutting down the engines, which was a serious mistake.

By now the flames were spewing from the after hatches and it was clear to Captain Miller and his crew that the *Annie Young* was doomed. Miller found himself the skipper of a burning ship running out of control on a stormy sea. Once his crew left the engine room there was no way to stop the ship until the fire went out in the boilers and stopped making steam. With the entire engine room burning, the chances of running out of steam right away seemed too much to hope for.

The problem was, launching lifeboats to make an escape from the burning ship was almost impossible while the vessel was under way. We will never know the thoughts that must have been racing through Miller's mind that morning as he assessed the dilemma he and his people were in. As long as Miller and his wheelsman could stay on the bridge, they kept the ship steering into the wind. This prevented the fire from spreading too quickly from the after part of the ship, and bought time for the crew members, who by now were huddling in the bow waiting for a miracle.

That miracle was in the works a few miles to the south. It was there that Captain Mitchell, aboard the steamer *Smith*, was watching the fire while his boat was speeding to the scene. When Mitchell saw that the *Young* was on fire, he ordered the tow lines cut and asked his engineer to crank the *Smith's* engines up to full speed.

Meanwhile, some of the crew members aboard the *Young* decided to launch a lifeboat. When the yawl was lowered from the davits, twelve men jumped into it. Three of them decided at the last minute to climb back to the ship, either because Miller ordered them back or else they realized the launch was foolhardy. The remaining nine dropped their boat into the water, but discovered that the force of the moving ship made it impossible for it to break away. The yawl was dragged like a wild, uncontrollable bronco in the *Young's* wake until the boat capsized and all nine men were tossed wildly into the sea to drown. Among the drowned men were George McManus of Port Huron, G. Conley of Collingwood, Ontario, J. Conally of Erie, J. Crosby of St. Catherines, Ontario, and J. Gallagher, no address given.

Finally the *Smith* caught up with the racing *Young*. Mitchell used every trick of seamanship he knew to pull his ship alongside the moving fireship so the trapped men could get away. They said he made three tries before he managed to get all fourteen sailors aboard the *Smith*. Mitchell then turned the *Smith* around and steamed south to Port Huron, probably to get medical attention for the burned sailors. Mitchell was decorated the following year for heroism.

Once he got to Port Huron, Captain Miller hired the tug *Kittie Haight* to take him back out to his burning command. By the time they arrived, the *Young* was stopped. She was still afloat, but the fire had consumed her to the point where there was nothing left to salvage. The tug stood by until the *Young* slipped under the rolling seas, making a great cloud of steam as she sank. The wreck still lies in the water near Lexington in about six fathoms of water.

# Death Cruise

Capt. Peter G. Minch, a prominent Cleveland shipping magnet, was proud of the newest addition to his fleet. The *Western Reserve,* built for Minch only two years earlier, was the largest and fastest of the six steamers he owned, and Minch liked to think she was among the finest ships on the lakes.

The three hundred-foot long, twenty-four hundred-ton *Reserve* was, indeed, among the largest and most powerful ships traversing the lakes in 1892. She was setting records in both speed and cargo carried, which only added to Minch's satisfaction. That was why Minch decided to take his family along for a summer cruise on the fleet flagship. The trip had been planned for weeks, and Minch, who spent his early years sailing the lakes, made it clear to friends he was looking forward to getting out of the Cleveland office and back on the water for this brief respite.

Traveling with Minch in the ship's guest staterooms were his wife, their ten-year-old son Charles, a daughter Florence, six; a sister-in-law, Mrs. Engleby, of Vermillion, Ohio, and her daughter, Bertha, of nine years.

Minch, who knew all too well the dangers of sailing late in the season when storms sweep the lakes, probably thought it safe to take his family on a cruise the last week in August. The weather was still warm and gales that time of the year were rare. Even if a storm did come, he was confident that the *Western Reserve* was a large and staunch enough vessel to carry them safely through it.

The ship, under command of Capt. Albert Myers, left Cleveland Sunday afternoon, August 28, under sunny skies. It was a gala occasion for the family as the big ship moved out into the placid waters of Lake Erie, her mighty engines throbbing under their feet. No one dreamed then that the ship was taking them on a horror cruise that would end in death and disaster. The *Western Reserve* was carrying water ballast for the trip up the lakes because her holds were empty. Plans

Only one crew member survived when the *Western Reserve* sank during a Lake Superior storm in 1892.

were to take on a load of iron ore at Two Harbors. All went well for the first two days. Everybody enjoyed the trip up the Detroit and St. Clair Rivers, where the *Reserve* traveled in a parade of steamers and barges working north, while a similar parade of vessels passed on their way south. These rivers, connecting Lakes Huron, St. Clair and Erie, have enjoyed the distinction of being among the busiest water thoroughfares in the world.

The cruise across Lake Huron was smooth, and by Tuesday afternoon, the big ship was locking through at Sault Ste. Marie, on her way into the deep cold waters of mighty Lake Superior. A brisk northwest wind was blowing and the seas were rolling as the *Western Reserve* steamed out into the lake that evening, but nobody worried. Captain Myers and Peter Minch both believed they had a staunch ship under their feet with all of the power needed to carry them safely through the worst of blows.

Harry Stewart, an Algonac, Michigan sailor who was the only survivor of the disaster to follow, later told what happened. He said the gale was growing in strength and the ship began to pound as soon as it passed Point Iroquois. "Everything went well until about sixty miles above Whitefish Point," Stewart said. "The first warning anyone on board had of impending danger was a terrible crash about 9:00 PM." The noise was the ship starting to break in two. As the great steel trusses snapped from the strain, the ship's main mast broke for some unexplained reason about half-way up, and plunged with ropes and pulleys to the deck, causing even more confusion as the passengers and crew came to the terrible realization of what was happening.

Both Myers and Minch knew the danger and they immediately ordered the ship's two lifeboats lowered. "She took in water fast from the start," Stewart said. Captain Minch, his family, and the officers and crew of the boat, to the number of seventeen got into the wooden yawl, and the others took to the metallic one. The *Reserve* sank in ten minutes, and before she had hardly gone out of sight the metallic yawl capsized." He said the wooden boat he was in was rowed to the overturned craft, but only two people, Carl Myers, the captain's son, and the ship's steward, Bert Smith, were pulled out of the water alive.

Thus it was that nineteen survivors, from an original number of twenty-seven passengers and crew members, started in the storm tossed open boat for Whitefish Point, about sixty miles to the southeast. Stewart said the wind was out of the west when they began the trip, but it later veered around to the north, helping to push the little boat along.

It was a terrible night of suffering as the waves tossed the boat and kept everybody drenched and cold. "The yawl was too small to hold the crew of nineteen. It was loaded down to within a foot of the water, and all night the spray kept breaking over us. We worked continuously bailing out the water with the only pail we had, and our hats. I remember Mrs. Minch hanging to one of the children and making a desperate effort for life. Then I heard Mr. Minch cry out, 'My God, there goes one of my children.'

"Carl Minch, the captain's son, and I were together. He asked me if I thought we could reach the shore. I said 'We will try.' While we were in the yawl a steamer passed us. I think it was the *Neshota*. We could see her red light, but they could not see us. We were to the westward of them. We shouted and screamed for half an hour, but in the roar of the storm they could not hear us. If we had a light they could have seen us. As a final resort we tried to burn one of the women's shawls, but it was too wet and would not light." Stewart said they kept their frail craft upright until about 7:00 AM the next day. The sun was up and land was in sight, only about a mile away, and everyone was beginning to feel hopeful. It was then that the final disaster struck. The boat got caught in a big breaker and capsized, tossing everyone without warning into the water. Stewart said that in the rush to escape the sinking ship, only a few people grabbed life jackets. He was not wearing one that night, but when the yawl went over, he somehow managed to grab a life jacket that someone had discarded in the bottom of the boat. It saved his life. "I got hold of it and put it on in the water," he said.

He said that all around him people struggled for a while in the water. He heard the cries of the women and children and the voices of the men as they tried to help one another. Later, everything got silent. It was then that Stewart began swimming for shore. It took him two hours but he made it. Sometime in mid-morning he staggered out of the water and then began a ten-mile trek east to the U. S. Life Saving Station.

# Surviving the Death Storm on Lake Erie

The story is a paradox. The steamer *Wocoken* was lost because the gale that blew on the night of October 14, 1893 used the shallow waters of Lake Erie to make waves with enough power to tear the ship apart. The three men who survived the wreck lived because the ship sank upright in the shallow lake, leaving her masts and rigging suspended above the water.

Thus it was that second mate J. P. Saph of Marine City, wheelsman J. H. Rice of Cleveland, and seaman Robert Crowding of Delaware were still alive when the storm abated the next day and Ontario life savers came from Port Rowan to rescue them. Saph said the fourteen other members of the crew apparently got swept overboard by a giant wave while they were trying to launch lifeboats.

The *Wocoken* was one of an estimated forty ships left wrecked or stranded by the storm that swept the lakes. At least sixty people were believed dead. The steamer, commanded by Capt. Albert Meswald of Marine City, was bound from Ashtabula, New York, to Milwaukee, Wisconsin, with eighteen hundred tons of coal. She stopped at Erie to pick up the barge *Joseph Paige,* and the two boats started west across Lake Erie, bound for the Detroit River.

The storm developed while the vessels were somewhere in the middle of the lake. It blew with such fury, Meswald decided to steam north and try to get on the lee side of Long Point. The *Wocoken* did not weather the storm well. The waves pounded her with such force the ship's windows were smashed, the railings were torn away, and even the heavy wooden hatches began to pound loose.

Meswald knew the boat was in serious trouble. He ordered the *Paige* cut free so the steamer could use all of its power to fight the storm. The *Paige* hoisted sail and scampered before the wind to the west end of Long Point, where the vessel anchored and rode out the gale. Even free of its consort, the *Wocoken* continued to take a beating. Some of the hatches got torn away by the wind and the seas began filling the ship as they washed over the deck. Meswald finally gave the order to abandon ship at about 10:00 PM. The crew was busy launching life boats when the ship was struck by a great wave that carried Meswald, his wife, Sarah, and twelve other sailors overboard. The same wave also sank the ship in one powerful stroke.

After the wave passed, only Saph, Rice and Crowding were left alive. All three swam to the ship's rigging and then hung there for the night until help arrived.

The *Wocoken* sank about two miles off the tip of Long Point in forty-eight feet of water. The fish tug *Bacon* later found four life boats with the *Wocoken's* name on them, plus the bodies of two sailors wearing life preservers. Also in the area were "miles of wreckage."

Also killed were Capt. David Jones, first mate, of Cleveland; chief engineer Michael Hinkelman, second engineer Matthew Hasler, firemen George Smith and John Hinkelman, steward Charles Minard, watchmen Henry Cranch and Edmund Eldridge, wheelsman William Eachl and deck hand Michael Kenney, all of Marine City, Michigan.

The *Wocoken* took all but three members of its crew to the bottom of Lake Erie when it sank in a gale in 1893.

# Why Did They Die?

There is a mystery surrounding the deaths of twenty-four sailors following the collision and sinkings of the steamers *Albany* and *Philadelphia* on fog shrouded Lake Huron. It happened during the early morning hours of November 7, 1893, after the two iron ships came together in a terrible crash about twenty miles off Pointe aux Barques.

Twenty-four men were crowded into one of the two lifeboats launched from the *Philadelphia* that morning. Their overturned yawl was found by members of the Pointe aux Barques life saving station. The body of one man, recovered a few hours later, indicated that something violent happened. The man's skull was crushed.

Was the frail lifeboat unknowingly struck by a passing ship in the darkness? Two other ships, the *City of Concord* and the *Cuba,* were known to have passed through the fog shrouded area that morning. There also was some speculation that the craft was hit by the still churning propellers of the sinking *Philadelphia.* But if either was true, why wasn't the lifeboat damaged? And why didn't the bodies of more of the victims show signs of injury?

As it was, all of the men were wearing life jackets. All were recovered by the life savers within twelve hours of the sinking. Eleven bodies were picked up at daybreak, only a few hours after the sinking. The water is cold in November, but sailors have been known to survive for many hours in the water if they are properly dressed. Why weren't some of the victims still alive?

Capt. A. E. Huff, skipper of the *Philadelphia,* told a court of inquiry at Tawas that he personally shoved the ill-fated lifeboat from the side of the sinking ship before he got away in the second lifeboat. He said everyone was all right when he last saw them. Two sailors interviewed by a *Port Huron Daily Times* reporter the day after the disaster told the same story. They said both lifeboats were successfully launched from the *Philadelphia,* one with twenty-three sail-

The iron steamer *Albany* sank first after colliding with the *Philadelphia* near Point aux Barques, Michigan, in 1893. Twenty-four sailors died when something happened to their lifeboat.

ors and the other with twenty-four aboard. They said Huff was the last man to get off. The men called to one another for a while in the fog. Later on, they said they did not hear from the other lifeboat any more. There was not a heavy sea running that day. They said they did not hear a sound of a collision or get any indication that anything was wrong on the other boat.

The collision occurred at about 2:00 AM. The *Philadelphia* was northbound with a load of coal and general merchandise for Chicago. The *Albany,* commanded by Capt. Angus McDonald, was steaming south with a load of grain. Sailors said the *Philadelphia* was "running under check," which means the speed was reduced and the crew was on alert because of the fog. "At about two o'clock we heard the whistle of a steamer dead ahead," one man said. "At the time we were blowing for signals, and it was only a few minutes before the *Albany* was in sight."

The men said the watchman on the *Albany* apparently spotted the *Philadelphia* at the same time. The wheelsmen from both boats put their helms hard to port, but it was too late. The bow of the twenty-five-year-old *Philadelphia* sliced deep into the port side of the *Albany*. From the nature of the

Twenty-four sailors mysteriously died when their lifeboat, launched from the *Philadelphia*, was flipped upside down on Lake Huron. The ship sank in a collision.

damage, it was obvious to everybody that the *Albany* would sink. "At the time we struck the *Albany* our engines were backing strong and we soon commenced to back away. We then turned around and ran along side of the *Albany,* taking off the crew and baggage," an unidentified sailor from the *Philadelphia* said.

Capt. Huff testified that he was in his cabin and didn't know anything was wrong until he heard the whistles. He said he didn't reach the deck until after the two vessels hit. Huff said he first thought the *Philadelphia* wasn't seriously hurt. He ordered a tow line hooked to the stricken *Albany* and began towing the listing vessel toward shore in the hope of running it aground before it sank.

The *Philadelphia's* sailors said that after running about thirty minutes with the *Albany* in tow, the collision bulkhead collapsed in their own ship and they realized that the *Philadelphia* also was sinking. Huff ordered the *Albany* cast adrift and proceeded to run the *Philadelphia* at full steam toward shore. The *Philadelphia* was settling quickly by the head, however, and the rising waters were threatening to put out the ship's fires. Huff gave up trying to save his ship and ordered the two lifeboats lowered. The lone lifeboat with twenty-three survivors made it safely to shore at Pointe aux Barques at about 7:30 AM.

# The Burning Roanoke

The steamer *Roanoke* seemed destined to burn. Flames swept the decks of the wooden hulled propeller twice. The final blaze destroyed and sank it August 7, 1894 while the ship was steaming from Port Huron to Washburn, Wisconsin, with a cargo of salt. She went down in one of the deepest parts of Lake Superior, about twenty miles off Fourteen Mile Point in about twelve hundred feet of water. There were no casualties with either fire.

The first burning occurred on about May 17, 1890, while the *Roanoke* was moored at the Northern Steamship Company dock in Buffalo. The blaze started in the hold, possibly from an overturned lantern, and spread to three hundred bales of jute butts loaded there. Dried jute burns hot, and within minutes flames were shooting up the midship hatch and spreading to the fresh painted woodwork between decks. The ship's gangways were open and a brisk offshore wind supplied all the oxygen the fire needed to race recklessly through the superstructure.

By the time the fire tug arrived, flames were flashing from the gangways at both ends of the ship. To save the dock, tugs towed the burning steamer to shallow water near the old life station. The fire was extinguished and by midnight, the smoking hulk was towed back to the dock once again. Her upperworks were ruined. Fire fighters continued pouring water into the smoldering jute for the rest of the night. The *Roanoke* was rebuilt and returned for another four seasons before the final fire consumed her.

Her master, Capt. Alonze Cox, said a defective lamp caused the final fire. He said the lamp exploded in the engine room. Within seconds the engine room floors, saturated with years of oil, coal dust and grime, were a myriad of dancing flames and the black gang fled for their lives. With the fire originating in the engine room, there was no chance for the crew to battle the flames. The ship's steam powered pumps were controlled from there. In fact, everybody fled so fast that

The *Roanoke* burned twice. The second fire sank the ship on Lake Superior in 1894.

nobody thought to shut down the engines. With the engines still running at full speed, the moving ship created wind that helped fan the fire.

The sailors formed a bucket brigade for a while, and one man, whose name was never told, braved the burning engine room to get one of the pumps operating. Cox said the fire fighting efforts were a lost cause. The fire started at about 10:30 PM, and by midnight, he said he had to give the order to abandon ship.

The lifeboats were dropped from the davits and the crew members sat helplessly in them, watching the fire consume and finally sink the ship that had been their home. The lifeboats drifted all night until the propeller *George Spencer* came along the next morning and picked everybody up.

The *Roanoke* had been on the lakes for twenty-seven years. She was built in Cleveland in 1867.

# Winter Fire

The watchman's fire in a galley stove was blamed for the fire that destroyed the passenger and freight propeller *Puritan* near Manistee on December 31, 1895.

The *Puritan* was tied up for the winter at Stokoe and Nelson's Dock at Oak Hill, south of town on Manistee Lake, after a busy season on a daily run between Chicago and Benton Harbor. The watchman, a man named Gallagher, was keeping a constant fire going in one of the galley stoves for warmth and to prepare his meals as he went about his daily routines.

Part of Gallagher's duties was to make repairs to the ship, getting her ready for spring. He was working in the hold at about 3:30 PM, repacking the bearings along the shaft at the stern pipe, when he heard noises and went forward to investigate. He was shocked to find that the ship was on fire and he was nearly trapped below deck. His normal exits were blocked by the flames, but Gallagher knew of a small emergency hatch in the stern. By wiggling through the hatch, he managed to escape to the nearby dock and call for help.

The upper cabins were making a spectacular show of fire and smoke when Manistee firefighters arrived with horse-drawn steam pumps and hoses. It was discovered that the fire could not be put out.

There were two reasons for this. The lake was frozen so harbor tugs with steam-powered pumps couldn't get close enough to attack the fire from the lake side. From land, firefighters found that the nearest fire hydrant was located on top of Oak Hill, about fifteen hundred feet away from the dock.

They did what they could. They strung all of their hoses on a single line from the hydrant, and then used the water to keep the fire from spreading to the docks and nearby lumber piles. No effort was made to save the ship. So it was that the *Puritan* burned until it sank in about forty feet of water three hours later. The hull and machinery were so badly damaged that the ship was scrapped.

The *Puritan* burned at its winter quarters near Manistee, Michigan, in 1895.

The *Puritan* had been on the lakes only eight years and had a reputation of being one of the fastest single screw propellers operating on Lake Michigan. The ship was built at Benton Harbor in 1887.

# Saving the Crew of the *E. B. Hale*

The wooden steamer *E. B. Hale* lies in the boneyard of sunken ships off Huron County Michigan's notorious Pointe aux Barques. The story of the *Hale's* sinking on October 8, 1897, and the crew's narrow escape to the steamer *Nebraska* during a raging southwest gale, is a true tale of horror on the Great Lakes.

Capt. James Lawless said he was bringing the ship from Lorrain, Ohio, to Milwaukee with more than a thousand tons of steel billets in the hold when it ran into the storm on Saginaw Bay. The gale put a strain on the heavily loaded twenty-three-year-old vessel. When off Point aux Barques a main steam pipe broke from the side of the boiler, filling the engine room with deadly steam and scalding water. Lawless said it was a miracle that Engineer John Cowley of St. Clair, Michigan, and his firemen escaped alive. Cowley was seriously injured but he survived.

Because of the steam and heated water, it was impossible for anyone to enter the engine room and make repairs. The engine was out of commission and the ship was tossing around at the mercy of the storm. Before long, the wooden hull began pulling apart from the strain. The steam-powered pumps couldn't be used so the sailors hoisted the old hand-operated pumps to the deck and tried to get the water out of the holds the hard way. "But the sea was running so high that the men were washed away," Lawless said. He said nobody was lost overboard, but there were some narrow escapes as sailors grabbed railings and ropes to keep from being swept off into eternity. They had to give up.

As the ship settled, things were looking very serious. Sometime in mid-day the *Nebraska* saw the *Hale's* distress signals and tried to help. An effort was made to run tow lines to the *Hale*, but the storm was blowing with such fury that the hawsers snapped. "Three times a line was thrown us from the *Nebraska*, but each time it broke owing to the violent lurching of the vessel. For several hours we were tossed about, the

**The sinking of the *E. B. Hale* in Lake Huron was a terrifying experience for the survivors in 1897.**

*Nebraska* lying close to, but being unable to aid us," Lawless said.

The crew of the *Hale* tried to abandon ship. A lifeboat was lowered, but it was smashed by the waves. The second boat was launched, but then the men couldn't get into it. Lawless said several men were tossed in the water by the storm, but then were miraculously rescued again. At last everybody got into the lone lifeboat and began pulling in the heavy seas for the waiting *Nebraska*. At first they were making no headway against the storm. The skipper of the *Nebraska* maneuvered his ship by backing up and then turning so that the lifeboat was shielded from the wind and waves.

The tired sailors finally managed to scramble aboard the waiting ship. Some of the survivors were badly bruised. Engineer Cowley had to be carried ashore when the *Nebraska* docked that night at Port Huron.

The *Hale* sank about thirty minutes after the crew left it. Some say it lies deep in about two hundred forty feet of water, about thirty-seven miles offshore.

# Overheated Boilers

Capt. C. O. Flynn inadvertently set fire to his own ship after running it aground on Lake Superior's Michigan Island. It hit a shoal just after midnight on June 4, 1899 while Flynn's command, the one hundred-foot coastal steamer *R. G. Stewart* was steaming through heavy fog at the western end of the lake.

The vessel was carrying three passengers and several head of cattle from Ontonagon to Duluth. After his ship struck, Captain Flynn spent the rest of the night on the bridge, keeping the crew hard at work, trying to work the vessel free under its own power.

What was so frustrating was that the *Stewart* moved a few feet every time the propeller would churn the waters, but it always stopped short of pulling free. As the night wore on, Flynn's patience grew thin. He ordered more steam. Then more. And still the *Stewart* remained caught on the reef. When the engineer complained that his engines were stretched to the limit, Flynn ordered him to put a blower on the ship's stack to force a hotter fire below.

In retrospect, Flynn admitted it was a mistake. "I went on deck to see if everything was ready to back again when the fireman shouted that the boat was on fire over the boilers," he said. The overheated engine room turned into an inferno in minutes, forcing the engine room crew to flee for their lives. The fire spread through the dried wood on the twenty-one-year-old ship so quickly that everybody scrambled for the lifeboat, not even taking time to save their personal belongings. Flynn said he left three hundred dollars in cash behind in his cabin.

Someone took time to drive the cattle into the lake. It might have been George McKenna, the ship's wheelsman, who was the last man to leave the burning ship. Witnesses said the fire was breaking through the deck under McKenna's feet as he prepared to lower himself into the lifeboat. Instead of climbing, McKenna jumped. He landed on the gunwale and

The *R. G. Stewart* was destroyed by fire while trying to back off a reef at Lake Superior's Michigan Island.

overturned the boat, spilling everybody in the water. Land was about a thousand feet away, so Flynn and five other men, Andrew O'Brien, McKenna, George Shortall, Fret Hantz and William Murphy tried to swim to shore. McKenna didn't make it. Flynn said McKenna and Hantz both went under. Shortall pulled Hantz ashore and revived him, but McKenna drowned.

Meanwhile, five other people were clinging to the overturned lifeboat, which was still tied to the burning ship. They said the fire got so hot they had to keep putting their heads and faces under water to keep from getting burned. Finally the fire burned the rope and the survivors floated to shore while still clinging to the boat.

# Part Three:
# New Century Terror
# 1900 to 1919

# The Engineer's Story

When the tug *Columbia* arrived at East Tawas the evening of May 24, 1901, she carried two bedraggled and still dripping sailors, both wrapped in blankets and riding in the warm cabin just over the engine room.

They were second engineer Thomas Murphy and deck hand George McGinnis, the only survivors of the wrecked steamer *Baltimore,* which broke up on a shoal that morning off Au Sable during a Lake Huron gale. The *Columbia* was out on the lake searching for a tow barge the tug lost in the storm when it came upon Murphy and McGinnis lashed to a piece of wreckage.

The two survivors were taken to private quarters in East Tawas. McGinnis appeared to be out of his head and Murphy was too exhausted at first to be questioned. Later, when Murphy gained strength, authorities were anxious to talk to him. Everybody wanted to know what happened to the *Baltimore* and her crew of thirteen other sailors.

He said the *Baltimore,* with Capt. M. H. Place at the helm, was bound from Loraine, Ohio, to Washburn, Wisconsin with a load of coal. "We had in tow a large steam drill and scow. When off Thunder Bay last night, Captain Place saw that the steamer was making bad weather, for the waves had smashed in the engineer's quarters and the washrooms (on the starboard side at the stern), and water was running into the hold."

Place decided the ship was taking too much of a beating on the course it was taking against the northeasterly gale. He turned the *Baltimore* southwest for Tawas, putting the wind at his stern. He hoped to anchor on the lee side of Tawas Point. Place lost his bearings in the storm and the darkness of the night, and ran the ship on a reef about a mile off Au Sable. Murphy said the ship immediately began to break up. "The seas broke over her . . . and carried away the deck house, then the after cabin and finally the smoke stack fell. Both

Only two crew members survived when the *Baltimore* struck a reef and broke up during a spring storm on Lake Huron.

rails were broken in two just aft of the forward deckhouse, and we knew it was only a few minutes before the steamer went to pieces."

Captain Place told the crew: "It is every man for himself now." Murphy said he saw the captain's wife, who was aboard as the ship's stewardess, standing next to the skipper. "The look of despair on her face was something I will never forget. It was awful. We took the captain's advice, and every man started to save himself as best he could. Some of the boys took to the rigging, but McGinnis and I lashed ourselves to a ringbolt in a piece of the after cabin, and we were washed overboard shortly afterward.

"The strain was too much for McGinnis, and he went crazy before we had been in the water very long. He tried to throw me off the wreckage, but I talked to him and encouraged him to hold on. Twice he got loose and tried to drown us both, but each time I succeeded in quieting him. I told him a boat was coming to take us off, and then I would get him tied fast again."

The men struggled in this way for six hours, battling the elements and each other to stay alive until help came. "Our wreckage was big enough to make a raft, but it was small, and the seas swept it constantly. The passenger steamer *City of Holland* passed by us, but we were too far away for her crew to see us. It made me feel pretty despondent for a time, for I was getting very weak and the seas broke over my head so as to drive the breath out of my body at times," Murphy said. At 2:00 PM, at about the time Murphy had given up hope of being rescued, the *Columbia* appeared, and the rescue was made.

Also lost in the wreck were first mate Michael Breathen; Capt. Louis Laffriner, an old shipbuilder who was aboard to make some internal renovations; John Delders, second steward; wheelsmen Edward Owen and C. W. Sears; watchmen George W. Scott and Herbert Winning; engineer Peter Marcoux; and fireman August Anderson.

The *Baltimore* was a new command for Captain Place. He had been master of the *Germanic* for several years, and after buying an interest in the *Baltimore,* was taking the ship out for one of the first trips of the season when it was lost. He brought his wife along as a member of the crew.

The *Baltimore* was originally named the *Escanaba* when built in 1881. She was two hundred feet long and carried about two thousand tons of freight. The hull was wood.

# The Haunting of Captain McLean

The freighter *John M. Nicol,* was in trouble. The ship had been fighting a fierce northeasterner on Lake Superior for several hours on the morning of September 16, 1901, and her seams were starting to open. The pumps were not keeping up with the water surging into the ship's vast hold.

At about dawn, Chief Engineer George E. Tretheway called Capt. William "Bill" McLean to the engine room to give him some more bad news. He showed McLean how the ship's steam pipes were starting to work loose because of the terrible wrenching and twisting of the iron hull. "This boat can't stand the strain much longer," Tretheway warned.

McLean had the *Nicol* steaming hard for Michigan's Keweenaw Peninsula, hoping to get to safety on the lee side of the land before his ship was lost. It was a race against time. McLean reasoned that if he got the *Nicol* close to land, he had the option of running the ship on the rocks to save it and the twenty-one members of his crew. He talked about this alternative plan to Tretheway.

This was McLean's state of mind at about 10:00 AM when the *Nicol* came on the steamer *Hudson* in a sinking condition about eight miles off Eagle River, Michigan. He couldn't believe his eyes. The *Hudson* was caught in the trough of the seas, her engines obviously cold because there was no smoke coming from the twin stacks, and the boat was listing hard to starboard. The seas were rolling over the sloping decks and men could be seen huddled together near the bow, clinging to the port railing.

It was obvious that the *Hudson* had developed engine trouble during the height of the storm, could not keep underway and fell off to the mercy of the wind and waves. Because of the severe rolling, its cargo of flax seed and wheat had shifted. By the time the *Nicol* arrived, the *Hudson* was within minutes of foundering.

The *Hudson* foundered with all hands during a gale on Lake Superior in 1901.

McLean had a terrible decision to make. Should he attempt to rescue those sailors aboard the *Hudson* at the risk of losing his own crippled ship? His choice was to save the *Nicol.* It was a decision that haunted McLean for the rest of his life. He was so shaken that he found it difficult to stop explaining his actions during the days that followed.

"We passed within a half mile of her and it was hard to go on and leave the men to their fate," he said after reaching Sault Ste. Marie two days later. "It was out of the question to stop, however much the call of humanity might demand it."

By the time he reached Detroit on September 23, McLean was going to great lengths to justify his actions. He told about the leaking steam pipes and the dash for safety behind the Keweenaw Peninsula. "It was a question of staying away and having one boat and one crew go down instead of running close and having two boats and two crews drowned in the storm," he said. "We were leaking badly, had three feet of water in our hold and the seas were washing us from stern to stem. We had two pumps and siphon working full blast, but still the water was gaining and there was twenty-five miles between us and the nearest point of shelter. In order to render any assistance it would have been necessary to run to the lee of (the *Hudson*) and get lines to the crew. To run to the lee of the *Hudson* would have meant to sink my own boat and sacrifice the lives of the twenty-one persons aboard her. One roll of the *Hudson* against the *Nicol* would have sent us to the bottom in five minutes. It was a terrible thing to see those men clinging there with not once chance in a thousand of ever getting away, and then have to pass them. But it would have been foolhardy to attempt to run close to her."

Because of the severe list, the men aboard the *Hudson* could not launch the lifeboats. The boats were still on the ship's davits when the *Hudson* sank. Thus it was that all twenty-five members of the *Hudson's* crew died with the ship that day. The dead included Capt. A. J. McDonald, first mate Charles Brooks, second mate Bert Gray, chief engineer Moses Trouton, second engineer George Vogt, and crew members Donald Glass, Peter Renning, Edward Miller, John Hughes, Heney Meyers and Neil S. Pearson.

Two regular crew members missed the trip. Thomas J. Reppenhagen, of Buffalo, the regular first mate, got Gray to replace him for the trip so he could be with his sick wife. Wheelsman Fred Peterson, who had been with the ship for seven years, decided for some unexplained reason to quit his job before the *Hudson* left Duluth on its trip of no-return.

# Top Heavy

The little steamer *H. Houghton* made headlines the day it turned over in the Detroit River and sank, drowning two crew members asleep below deck.

The accident happened at 4:15 AM on September 9, 1902. The *Houghton* had arrived at Detroit only a few hours before with its hull riding deep in the water from the weight of a load of crushed stone shipped from Marblehead, Ohio. The stone not only filled the hold, but it was stacked high on the deck. It was obvious that the owners had this one hundred and twenty-six-foot vessel loaded far beyond the hundred and fifty tons it was designed to carry. To make matters worse, Capt. William Deeg said the ship passed through a heavy rain on Lake Erie, and the water was absorbed by the stone, adding still more weight to the deck load. The ship was top heavy.

Second engineer D. Anderson was up and stirring early that morning, which turned out to be a good thing. He noticed that the *Houghton* was taking on a list that was getting worse by the moment. He stood on the deck, jerking the steam whistle cord to wake up the crew and get everybody scrambling for the dock. His actions saved Deeg, the ship's cook, Mrs. Mary Neville, and five others.

Deeg said he was helping Mrs. Neville step from the deck when the hawsers broke from the strain. The steamer then rolled on its side and sank in twenty-two feet of water. Sailors Edward Close of Harbor Beach and William Daniels, address unknown, never got out.

The *Houghton* was raised and repaired. The ship was sold to Winaford L. Emery in 1914 and Emery used it to haul sand.

The boat was sold to the Service Gravel Company of Marysville in 1926 and converted to be a sandsucker. It was ending a first season in this new role when a fire destroyed it on November 20. The steamer was under command of Capt. Robert B. Young when it burned and sank in the North Chan-

**Two died when the stone laden *Henry Houghton* capsized and sank at Detroit in 1902.**

nel of the St. Clair Flats, just below Algonac. Young and thirteen other crew members escaped in a lifeboat.

# Chasing the *Queen*

Captain McKenzie was perplexed. Here he was, early in the day on August 20, 1903, driving his ship, the steamer *Codorus,* at top speed through rough seas on Lake Erie, trying to rescue people aboard the sinking ore carrier *Queen of the West,* but the sinking ship was not cooperating. The boat was dashing along with her engines operating at full speed. The *Codorus* was involved in the strange chase because McKenzie answered a call of distress from the *Queen's* whistle.

Any sailor knows that pulling a ship alongside another when both vessels are moving takes daring and a lot of skill. As McKenzie watched the fleeing ship with his glass, he saw something that made him decide to try the rescue anyway. "When we came near I could see the crew on the deck with life preservers on. Just before we reached her a big sea washed over her decks and carried away the two little daughters of Chief engineer (G. H. ) Drouillard. They appeared to be gone, but when the water cleared away, I caught sight of them on the other side of the deck, where the water had carried them."

McKenzie was probably thinking the *Queen's* master, Capt. S. B. Massey of Ogdensburg, New York, had lost his senses. "She was running away from us with full steam," he said. As the *Codorus* gained and the two racing ships drew close, McKenzie said it was obvious that the crew on the *Queen of the West* needed help and they needed it quickly. He said the seas had washed away the lifeboats and several people were on deck, clinging to anything they could hang onto, as the charging boat settled lower and lower in the water.

At last the *Codorus* was alongside. Everybody jumped for their lives. It was a dangerous moment. Wheelsman Patrick Maloney of Baltimore slipped and fell between the two ships but was pulled out again before he was crushed to death. As it was, the boats squeezed against him enough to break three ribs. He was later hospitalized. Soon the fifteen sailors and two daughters of the engineer, identified as Jennie and Mabel, were off the sinking *Queen.* Drouillard, who stayed alone in

The captain of the *Queen of the West* was afraid to stop his sinking ship so the crew could be taken off.

waist deep water in the engine room to feed the fires, was the last man to leave the ship. The *Queen* continued her strange voyage into oblivion for a while, and the *Codorus* followed until the sinking boat lost steam and foundered. After that the *Codorus* turned for Fairport, Ohio.

Massey had some explaining to do. "I feared that if I did (stop), we would get into the trough of the sea and sink at once," he answered.

The *Queen of the West* was making a short trip from Cleveland to Erie on Lake Erie when it foundered a few miles off Fairport. It was carrying fifteen hundred tons of iron ore.

# Loss of the *Iron Chief*

A ship's graveyard lies just off the northeast tip of lower Michigan's little peninsula, within sight of the old lighthouse at Lake Huron's Pointe aux Barques. When the weather is good, sport divers like to visit some of the better-known wrecks, all bunched within a few miles of one another. They are deep dives, many of them up to a hundred and fifty feet down, so only the most experienced divers dare to visit them.

Among these wrecks is the *Iron Chief,* a two hundred twelve-foot wooden hulled steamer that met its fate on October 3, 1904. Built as a schooner twenty-three years earlier at Detroit, the *Iron Chief* was later converted to be a steam barge. The steamer never lost the grace it had as a sailing ship, and the boat carried four masts until the day it went to the bottom.

The final trip into Lake Huron began like all the others. The *Iron Chief,* commanded by Capt. U. S. Cody, was towing the barge *Iron Cliff* north from Port Huron to Duluth; both vessels laden with coal. They ran into rough weather when off Saginaw Bay. It wasn't a serious storm and Cody wasn't concerned. He knew the *Iron Chief* was an old ship, but she had weathered this kind of sea before.

What Cody didn't count on, however, was an accident. The ship's stern pipe, sometimes called a stuffing box, located where the propeller shaft passes through the hull, failed and the ship developed a serious leak. Chief engineer Charles Steadman and one of his helpers made an effort to repair the leak from inside the ship, but it was not successful. They were driven from the area, and later from the engine room as the ship flooded.

Once the fires in the boiler were extinguished the *Iron Chief* was adrift without power. The barge *Iron Cliff* cut its tow lines and set sail for Alpena. Because of the storm, the vessel did not turn around and pull along side the sinking steamer to take off the crew.

The steamer *Andrew Carnegie* came on the *Iron Chief* at about 11:00 PM. Capt. John McArthur, of Port Huron, mas-

The *Iron Chief* sprung a leak and sank off Lake Huron's Point aux Barques.

ter of the *Carnegie,* put a tow line to the vessel and tried to pull it to Harbor Beach. Progress was slow because the half sunken *Iron Chief* was riding low in the water and the seas were rough. By 7:00 AM the next day, as the two boats were passing Point aux Barques, the *Iron Chief* called it quits. McArthur saw that the ship was lost. He cut the tow line and pulled his boat along side the *Iron Chief* in time to take off the crew of thirteen sailors before the vessel disappeared under the waves.

Divers say the *Iron Chief* broke up when it hit bottom stern first. The superstructure broke off and floated away, the ship's sides buckled and exploded outward. Her decks were torn apart and the timbers were tossed in all directions. The cargo of coal is still there, with ribs of the old ship sticking up through it. The boiler rests alone on the bottom. The *Iron Chief's* anchor is on display at the Grice Museum at Harbor Beach.

# Reddy Was a Hero

Coal passer William "Reddy" Holloran saved the day for his fellow shipmates when fire broke out on the steamer *Germanic*. It happened at about 3:00 AM on November 6, 1904, while the ship was hard aground at the head of Stag Island, on the St. Clair River near Marine City, Michigan.

The *Germanic*, under command of Capt. James Murphy, had dragged her anchor while waiting out a heavy fog and drifted into the island two days earlier. When tugs couldn't pull the ship free, extra workers were hired to help the crew shovel the cargo of coal to the *Active*, a shallow draft boat called a lighter, which was moored alongside.

The men were exhausted from the hard work and were sound asleep when the fire started from an unknown cause in the engine room. Fortunately, Holloran was awakened by the crackling of burning wood. He woke three other sailors, Bob Friedenberg and Henry Flentche, both firemen, and coal passer James Doris, sleeping in quarters below the deck aft. As the four tried to exit by the narrow stairway leading to the main deck, they discovered it filled with smoke and fire. For a while it appeared that the men were trapped below deck. Holloran remembered a scuttle hatch leading to the fantail. He found it, got it open, and everybody escaped.

Other crew members also found themselves in grave danger. Chief Engineer Anton Rudd woke to find his bed on fire. He got away but was badly burned. Everybody escaped to the deck of the *Active*, then cut the mooring lines, so the lighter could drift away from the burning steamer.

The tug *Colton*, operated by Capt. Joseph Hayes, saw the flames and put some fire hoses on the blaze. The *Germanic* was burning so hot that the flames spread to the tug. Hayes gave up on the *Germanic* and steamed away, with the fire hoses turned on the *Colton's* own decks instead. The coal in the ship burned for days before the fire was finally out. The hull later was towed to Midland, Ontario, where it was rebuilt in 1909 as the *Reliever*. That ship caught fire later the

**The crew narrowly escaped when the *Germanic* burned on the St. Clair River in 1904.**

same year at Methodist Point, on Georgian Bay. This time her registry was closed for good.

# Saga of the *Olive Jeannette*

When the steamer *Iosco* and her tow, the schooner *Olive Jeannette* foundered with all hands during a Lake Superior gale in 1905, lakemen wondered if the schooner was cursed. The *Jeannette* was involved in an almost identical disaster, that time involving the *Iosco's* sister ship, the *L. R. Doty*, during a storm on Lake Michigan in 1898.

That time the *Doty* sank with all hands, but the *Jeannette* was set adrift and survived to sail again. Seventeen sailors perished when the *Doty*, owned by the Cuyahoga Transit Company of Chicago, disappeared in the gale on October 25. Capt. David B. Cadotte, master of the *Jeannette*, was credited with bringing his schooner through the storm against almost impossible odds.

His story is among the best in the annuals of lake lore. It seems that the *Doty* was steaming north from Chicago to Midland, Ontario, with a load of corn, and had the *Jeannette* in tow, when the two vessels got caught in a severe northerly gale. Cadotte said the *Jeannette* broke her tow line at about 5:00 PM while a few miles northeast of Milwaukee. The *Doty* didn't stop, and was last seen steaming north into the teeth of the gale. He said everything appeared to be all right aboard the steamer at that time.

Cadotte ordered some canvas spread and he sailed the *Jeannette* before the wind toward Racine. It was a long and dangerous trip, and waves continually rolled over the stern of the schooner, drenching the sailors working on the deck, but she was making progress. At about 11:00 PM, with the Racine light in sight and safety only about an hour away, the ship's steering fouled and the schooner fell off into the trough of the sea. The monster waves began rolling over the deck from the side and they swept the ship clean. Before long Cadotte said the waves carried away the steam pumps, deck housing and everything that wasn't fastened down.

While all this was going on, the crew struggled against the storm to toggle up the steering chains so the ship could make another try for port. In the meantime, the gale blew the boat past Racine. When the rudder was again under control, Cadotte decided the next possible chance for shelter would be Chicago. It wasn't long before the constant buffeting by wind and sea against the stern wrecked the steering again. This time it could not be fixed. The *Jeannette* was again at the mercy of the storm. She broached and drifted for the rest of the night, taking a terrible beating. The ten sailors aboard the schooner spent an ugly night at sea, clinging to the ship but finding no place to get dry, no shelter from the gale. Surprisingly, the hatches survived the ordeal. They stayed in place, and that saved the ship. A steamer found the *Jeannette* adrift a few miles off Chicago the next day and towed her into port.

In the meantime, the *Doty* turned up missing. The steamer was declared lost on October 27 after the tug *Prodigy* found wreckage from a steamer about twenty-five miles off Kenosha, Wisconsin. The debris included pieces of deck, a pole mast, cabin doors, stanchions and part of the steering pole from the bow. The exact location of the *Doty* was never known. It was theorized that the ship developed engine trouble and drifted off in the trough of the seas. The *Doty* had a full cargo, and because it had a low freeboard, it probably took a deadly pounding from the seas that struck her broadside. If the hatch covers failed, the ship probably filled and sank.

Seventeen sailors died on the *Doty*. They included Capt. Christopher Smith of Port Huron, chief engineer Thomas Abernethy of Port Huron, assistant engineer Charles Odette of Cleveland, first mate Harry Sharpe of Detroit, steward L. Goss of Bay City, second mate W. J. Hosie of Detroit, oiler Wallace Watkins, cook W. J. Scott, watchman Charles Barrie, wheelsmen Peter G. Peterson and Albert Nelson, firemen Joseph Fitzsimmons and J. Howe, and deck hands F. Parmuth, C. Curtis, William Ebert, Pat Ryan, Frank Burke and T. Trainer.

The story continues four years later.

The *Jeannette* was lost on September 3, 1905, when it foundered with the steamer *Iosco* off Huron Islands, on Lake Superior. They said the *Iosco* was a carbon copy of the *Doty*.

**The four masted schooner *Olive Jeannette* sank with the steamer *Iosco* in 1905. Some sailors wondered if the schooner was cursed.**

When the two vessels were both in the water, experienced lakemen had to look twice to tell one from the other.

Both the *Iosco* and the *Jeannette* were laden with iron ore when they left Duluth bound for Buffalo. The storm hit them when they were in the middle of Lake Superior. There were no survivors so nobody knows what happened. The *Iosco* apparently went down first because a lighthouse keeper at Huron Island said he didn't see a steamer when he watched the *Olive Jeannette* founder about four miles north of the island at about 4:00 PM. He said the big four-masted schooner had jib and foresail set and was nearly waterlogged minutes before it sank.

The tug *D. L. Hebard* discovered wreckage, including life preservers marked *Iosco* near the island the next day, so it was believed both vessels foundered in the same area. Twenty seven sailors died in the two boats. The *Iosco* carried a crew of nineteen while the *Jeannette* had eight men aboard.

On the *Iosco* were Capt. Nelson Gonyaw of Bay City, chief engineer Frank M. Gordon of Cleveland, mate F. H. Griffin, second engineer George Shawn, oiler Martin W. Stanton, steward W. B. Barnes, assistant steward Mrs. Barnes, watchmen Arthur Roberts and Robert Ray, wheelsmen Matthew Cummings and John Brooks, firemen Charles Graff, August

The *Iosco* foundered with all hands in a gale on Lake Superior. The schooner *Olive Jeannette*, which was in tow, also was sunk.

The *L. R. Doty*, a sister ship to the *Iosco*, sank in Lake Michigan in 1898. The *Doty* also had the *Olive Jeannette* in tow.

Frank, Andrew Murphy and A. McDonald, and deck hands J. Smith, M. J. Martin, Victor Glamlin and Alfred Lewis.

The lost crew on the *Jeannette* included Capt. McGreery of Buffalo, mate J. Waller, engineer J. M. Dunn, steward William Johnson, and sailors G. Bohlin, J. Ellison, James Gilbarson and Charles Showman.

Both ships were owned by W. A. Hawgood and Company of Cleveland.

# Lake Huron's Ghost Ship *Kaliyuga*

When Simon Langell built his big new steamer at the St. Clair shipyards in 1887, he named it *Kaliyuga,* an ancient name that was supposed to mean "age of iron." It was an unusual name for this steamer, because, while it was built early in the age of iron ships, the *Kaliyuga* was among the last of the wooden hulled steamers. Had it been made of iron, perhaps it might have been strong enough to withstand the storm that claimed her. The ship foundered with all hands somewhere in Lake Huron during the big storm of October 19, 1905.

That storm, with winds clocked at seventy-two miles an hour, was among the worst in terms of lives and property lost on the Great Lakes. An estimated forty sailors perished and the *Kaliyuga* was one of some twenty-seven ships that were either sunk or driven on the rocks.

The boat was on its way down the lakes from Marquette, loaded with iron ore for Cleveland when it disappeared. She locked through at Sault Ste. Marie early Thursday morning and was leaving the lower St. Mary's River about the time the gale was starting to build on Lake Huron. The *Kaliyuga* was last seen by the crew of the steamer *Frontenac* at about 4:00 PM off Presque Isle. Capt. F. L. Tomkin, who was in his first year as a lakes pilot, was following the old, prescribed rules for riding out a storm. The gale was pounding his ship from the northeast, and he had her bow pointed into the wind to offer the least resistance to both wind and wave.

Capt. John Duddleson, skipper of the steamer *L. C. Waldo,* reported seeing the *Kaliyuga* about dusk on Thursday, still steaming east against the wind between Middle and Thunder Bay Islands. Duddleson may have been the last person to see the ill-fated vessel. He said that at about 2:00 AM Friday the wind shifted and blew a "terrible sea" from the northwest. Sailors who know the lakes say those wind shifts on Lake Huron can do terrible things to a ship. Waves strike from one direction while wind is attacking from another. Sometimes even the waves can build from two different directions.

The strain has broken the backs of even the steel hulled boats over the years. Nothing more was heard from the *Kaliyuga,* and by the following Monday, her owners, the St. Clair Steamship Company of Cleveland, reported her missing. An extensive search was launched. On October 26 the steamer *Lillie Smith* found a pilothouse and sections of cabin floating in Georgian Bay. The nameboard on the pilothouse said *"Kaliyuga."* Bodies washed ashore south of Kincardine and at Port Elgin, Ontario.

The official record places the wreck somewhere off Presque Isle, but Duddleson's sighting indicated the ship was farther south and west. The *Kaliyuga's* exact location has never been found. She joined the so-called ghost ships, that "fell through the crack" and were never seen again.

Seventeen other sailors died with the *Kaliyuga.* Among them were: Charles Simmons, first mate; Charles J. Murphy of Milwaukee, second mate; Charles A. Sharpe of Cleveland, chief engineer; Ernest E. Moder, second engineer; Mr. and Mrs. Harry Lefianne, stewards; Thomas Carr, wheelsman; Thomas Wright of Cleveland, watchman; George E. Foster, watchman; Charles Beaugrand, oiler; Thomas H. Sullivan, fireman; F. McKay, fireman; John Ross, John Rush and John Yolter, seamen.

**The ill-fated *Kaliyuga* before its launch at St. Clair, Michigan, in 1887. The boat foundered on Lake Huron in 1905.**

# Last Meal on the *Mills*

Chief engineer Ephriam J. Moore and his wife, Melissa, of Port Huron, were enjoying a noon lunch together in their cabin aboard the steamer *Nelson Mills.*

The *Mills* was steaming up the St. Clair River, approaching Port Huron, where Melissa planned to get off the boat. She was finishing a pleasure trip on the boat with her husband to Cleveland and back. She didn't know it, but she was never going to see Port Huron. She was one of two people to die the afternoon of September 6, 1906, in a collision three miles below St. Clair, Michigan.

The *Mills,* commanded by Capt. Daniel Warwick, was bound from Cleveland, to Algoma Mills, Ontario, with the barge *Alex Anderson* in tow. Both vessels were loaded with coal. As the boats slowly worked their way against the river current, they met the downbound propeller *Milwaukee,* carrying passengers and light freight bound for Buffalo. Witnesses said the *Milwaukee's* whistle sounded and the *Mills* answered with a single blast as the two vessels approached each other, each taking the starboard side of the river. Captain Osborn, master of the *Milwaukee,* left the bridge to get his dinner. All seemed well.

Something went wrong with the steering chains on the *Mills* as the two boats drew near. The wooden-hulled boat went out of control, veered unexpectedly to port and slid directly across the *Milwaukee's* bow. The two ships hit almost bow on, the heavier *Milwaukee* driving her stem deep into the starboard side of the ill-fated *Mills.* The time was 12:10 p.m.

Moore and his wife were almost knocked to the deck from the jolt. Moore knew immediately what happened and he took steps to lead Melissa to safety. He put a life jacket on her, led her out on deck, and when he saw that the *Mills* was sinking fast by the bow, he told her to jump with the other crew members into the river. For some unexplained reason,

**Two people died when the *Nelson Mills* sank in a collision on the St. Clair River in 1906.**

Moore left Melissa there on her own. Melissa was apparently more afraid of the water than she was of her chances aboard the sinking ship because she didn't jump. She was last seen clinging to the steamer as it sank in about forty feet of water. Her body was later recovered in the wreckage of the cabin, which broke away from the hull and floated down river.

Also killed was wheelsman James Barber of Port Sanilac. Details of Barber's death were not recorded. He apparently drowned after jumping in the river.

The *Milwaukee* dropped anchor and sent a boat to recover survivors in the water. Those rescued included second engineer Gib Edmondson, fireman D. Moore and wheelsman Joseph Baird, all of Marysville, Michigan, and cook Charles Nicholai of Port Huron.

Later the *Milwaukee* continued on to Buffalo, even though she was badly crushed in the bow.

The *Mills* was built in Vicksburg, Michigan as a barge. The deck and cabins were added and the ship was converted to a propeller in 1871. She was a small vessel, measuring only a hundred sixty-four feet in length.

# Burning of the *Charles A. Street*

The burned-out hull of the freighter *Charles A. Street* still lies just under the surface of Lake Huron, near the little Michigan settlement of Richmondville, where it sank in 1908. The ship burned there on July 21 after Capt. William R. Dunn and his crew of thirteen sailors drove it aground during an exciting run for their lives.

The steamer delivered coal at Sturgeon Bay and was returning to Toledo empty with three empty barges in tow when the fire broke out at about 11:00 PM. "Before we were aware of it, the after cabins were all on fire, and the (life) boats were enveloped in flames," Dunn later said.

Dunn said the first reaction was to try to fight the fire. It was soon evident that the wooden hulled ship was lost. He said the crew cut the tow lines to the barges *J. Godfrey, J. B. Lozen* and *William McGregor,* and then made steam in a dra-

The *Charles A. Street* burned and sank in Lake Michigan. The wreck lies near Richmondville.

matic dash toward the shore. Even though the engineer fled the stokehole, an unidentified fireman stayed on the job, feeding coal to the furnaces while the fire burned hot over his head. Dunn said the man narrowly escaped the fire after the *Street* crunched to a halt on a reef.

In the meantime, sailors on deck were busy making rafts out of doors and pieces of wood torn from the ship. The lifeboats were burned so they knew they needed some other way of getting ashore when they abandoned ship. Even though the steamer was aground, the water was still too deep for the crew to wade ashore.

Things appeared bad for the men as the fire worked its way forward. Then, at the last moment, Captain Forton, master of the barge *Godfrey,* pulled alongside with a lifeboat and took everybody off. Dunn said Forton's crew had to row about three miles to reach the stricken ship, but they made it on time.

# Strange Disappearance of the *Soo City*

After a successful twenty-year career on the Great Lakes, the ornate passenger steamer *Soo City* met its end in a cloak of mystery on the North Atlantic.

Nineteen sailors died when the ship disappeared sometime between November 14 and December 4, 1908, while making a trip from Quebec toward the Atlantic Seaboard. The first that anyone knew something happened to the ship was when wreckage started washing ashore December 4 near North Sidney, Nova Scotia.

The *Soo City* had been a popular excursion liner before the owners, the Indiana Transportation Company, sold the boat to Felix Jackson of Velasco, Texas. Jackson planned to put the ship in service along the Texas coast on the Gulf of Mexico.

Capt. F. V. Dority of Milwaukee, Wisconsin, was in command when the *Soo City* steamed off on her final voyage through the lakes. She left Michigan City, Indiana on November 1, and reached Ogdensburg, New York, on November 11. There Dority turned the helm to Capt. John G. Dillon, Brooklyn, New York, who was assigned to take the ship out the St. Lawrence River and then south along the Atlantic coast to Velasco.

The other crew members remained aboard for the trip. They included second mate Angus McIntyre of Chicago; first mate Charles L. Warwick, Michigan City; second engineer N. J. Duncan, Chicago; purser James Anderson, Montague, Michigan; oilers Frank Kelly, Alpena, Michigan, and George Brown, Chicago; firemen Frank Schwimm, Michigan City, and Samuel Olebsky, Chicago; coal passer E. L. Weaver, Dowagiac, Michigan; and cooks Max Sanders and Charles Warner, both of Chicago.

After taking on coal at Quebec, the vessel started off on a trip down the St. Lawrence River and was never seen again. The *Soo City* was first thought to have foundered in a violent winter storm that swept the Great Lakes and went

**After twenty years on the lakes, the *Soo City* disappeared under mysterious circumstances on the North Atlantic.**

east to the North Atlantic on December 1 and 2. Several vessels on the lakes, including the steamer *Tampa,* were sunk or driven ashore and lives were lost. When life belts began drifting ashore with the names of both the *S. S. Stanley* and *Soo City,* people theorized a collision at sea.

The mystery deepened after the *Stanley,* a Canadian icebreaker, was found safe at Charlotte Town, Prince Edward Island. Nobody could explain how the life belts got mixed up with those of the stricken *Soo City.* No bodies came ashore.

Sailors also wondered why the *Soo City* was still in the North Atlantic on December 1, because she sailed from Quebec on Nov. 14. They said the boat was expected to reach its destination at Texas in about ten days.

The only way it could have happened, they reasoned, was if the ship became disabled and drifted for several days until the storm sank it. The mystery was never solved because there were no survivors and the wreck has never been found.

# What Happened to the *Clemson?*

The sinking of the steel freighter *D. M. Clemson* remains among the many mysteries of the lakes. The ship disappeared on Lake Superior with all twenty-four hands during a winter gale on November 30, 1908.

There were no survivors to tell the story, but the lake left a few clues. Debris and the body of a lone crew member, watchman Simon Dunn, washed ashore at Crisp Point, about eighteen miles west of Whitefish Point where the *Clemson* was last seen during a blinding snowstorm. Dunn was wearing a life preserver. Later, pieces of the ship's cabin, twenty-three hatch covers and three more bodies were found farther west, between Crisp and Vermilion Points, off Grand Marais. One of the bodies was that of second mate Charles Woods, of Marine City.

Authorities speculated that the hatch covers failed the *Clemson* during the gale, causing water to flood the hold and sink the ship somewhere off Grand Marais. Yet others said they thought the steamer broke in two and sank quickly. They said the force of compressed air in the hold of the sinking ship would have caused the hatch covers to blow free at the same time. That few bodies were recovered supports the theory that the *Clemson* sank without warning. Most crew members were caught inside the ship and they didn't have time to put on life preservers.

The *Clemson* was under the command of Capt. S. R. Chamberlain, Duluth, when it sank. The ship cleared the Sault Ste. Marie locks at 9:30 AM on November 30 and then headed north to meet the northwest gale that claimed her. It was steaming up the lakes from Lorain, Ohio, on what was to have been a final trip of the season.

Other crew members lost included first mate W. E. McLeod, Duluth; chief engineer J. J. McCoy, Duluth; assistant engineers Lee Cunningham, Toledo and Guy Webb, Duluth; steward Bert Balfour and assistant steward Steve Vollman, both of Marine City.

Twenty-four sailors perished when the *D. M. Clemson* disappeared on Lake Superior in 1908.

# The Ship That Shot the Rapids

Everybody knows that the canal and locks were built at Sault Ste. Marie in 1855 to allow lake vessels to pass from Lake Superior to Lake Huron. What few people know, however, is that the locks are there to accommodate an eighteen-foot drop in the water level between Lake Superior and the bottom of the St. Mary Falls.

With that much of a drop, one can imagine the rush of water that would result if a set of the giant lock gates should suddenly become dislodged, allowing a free flow of water from Superior into the river below. That is what happened on June 9, 1909, while the passenger liner *Assiniboia* was standing in the Canadian lock. She was downbound that day with about a hundred passengers aboard.

When the traffic was heavy vessels sometimes went through in pairs. The *Assiniboia* went in the lock first and was waiting for the ore carrier *Crescent City* to enter behind her. According to the U. S. Army Corps of Engineers report, the steamer *Perry G. Walker* was approaching the locks from below at the same time, jockeying for a position in the upbound lock. Something went wrong and the *Walker* rammed the lower lock gate at about 1:00 PM.

The blow broke the gate miter and the giant steel gate, which was holding back all of Lake Superior at that moment, broke away, allowing an avalanche of water to roar through the canal. The force of the water carried both the *Assiniboia* and *Crescent City* through the lock with great speed.

Passengers aboard the *Assiniboia* were jostled as the big boat suddenly "shot the rapids," banging against the side of the *Walker* and finally ramming her bow into the side of the steamer *Empire City*. The collisions put a hole in the *Assiniboia's* bow and dents in the sides of both the *Walker* and *Empire City*. The *Crescent City* also was damaged.

Surprisingly, nobody was reported hurt. The lock was out of service for twelve days, until June 21.

The *Assiniboia* was a newcomer to the lakes when she shot her way through the locks. She was built in Govan, Scotland, in 1907 and came across the Atlantic Ocean that year under her own power.

The boat's length of three hundred and thirty-six feet made it too long to squeeze through the Welland Canal locks, so the owners cut it in half and then towed the two parts through the locks to Buffalo, where they were rejoined.

The *Assiniboia* served the lakes as a passenger vessel, and later a freight hauler, until 1967. She was sold the following year to a Lambton, Ontario businessman who planned to convert the vessel to a floating restaurant. The sixty-one-year-old ship was towed back down the St. Lawrence River and docked at West Duptford Township, New Jersey. There it burned and sank on November 9, 1969. The charred wreck was raised in 1970 and towed to Bordentown, New Jersey, for scrapping.

A hundred passengers held on for their lives when the *Assiniboia* raced through a broken lock at Sault Ste. Marie.

# Bad Years for the *Badger State*

If records were kept for the volume of freight and passengers hauled on the Great Lakes, the propeller *Badger State* might hold one. The two hundred ten-foot steamer competed on the route between Buffalo and Chicago in 1862. The ship was still going strong forty-seven years later, although it was reduced to the role of a tired lumber hooker, when destroyed by a fire at Marine City, Michigan, on December 6, 1909.

Four years before it burned, the *Badger State* fell into a period of disrepute. Still rigged as a passenger and freight hauler, the vessel was chartered by a Detroit gambling syndicate and was refurbished as a floating pleasure palace. The syndicate had been reeling under tough new Michigan laws that made it illegal to bet money on sports events, including boxing and horse racing. To get around the law, the mob planned to anchor the ship just outside of state jurisdiction, then ferry customers to and from the *Badger State's* decks. The upper decks were fitted out with gambling paraphernalia, including a restaurant and bar. The main piece of equipment was a giant blackboard, on which the winners of the various races and sports events were recorded. The information was to be transmitted to the ship on the very latest invention in 1905, the wireless telegraph.

The ship anchored off the head of Belle Isle, in the Detroit River, where the illicit business went on under the noses of state and city authorities. No law could be found to stop the gambling, so for a few weeks, the *Badger State* was the center of much activity. Then something happened. An unidentified man filed a complaint with the district attorney's office that the floating gambling house with its trailing cables was a menace to navigation. The government agreed. The *Badger State* was seized and put out of business.

The ship remained docked at Detroit until sometime in 1909, when the government sold it to the Alpena Cedar and Lumber Company, and the boat was converted for the lumber business.

**The *Badger State* fell on hard times when it was used as a floating gampling center on the Detroit River.**

The *Badger State* wasn't on this new job very long before it was destroyed by fire. It happened at night, while the ship was moored with several other vessels at the Marine City dock. Captain Lennon, who was the only person aboard that night, escaped, but he made a hasty flight. With normal exits blocked by the flames, Lennon jumped to the deck of a ship tied alongside.

To save the other vessels and the dock, the mooring lines were cut and the burning boat was set adrift in the St. Clair River. It floated to the Canadian side, where it ran aground and then burned to ruin.

# Erie Horror Story

Chief engineer A. Welch's story of survival on the burning freighter *Clarion* was enough to send a cold chill down the spine of the most hardened Great Lakes sailor. Welch and five other men found themselves trapped aboard the burning ship, in the night, with a serious winter gale blowing, in the middle of Lake Erie, and without a lifeboat.

It happened the night of December 8, 1909.

Welch told of leading the small band of men in a four-hour fight for their lives, and successfully holding the fire back until the steamer *L. C. Hanna* came alongside to take them off. "The intense heat had driven us to about the limit of endurance when we were rescued," he said. The other sailors, identified as second engineer John Graham, firemen Harry Murray, Theodore Larson and Joseph Baker, and cook Michael Toomey, praised Welch for his leadership during the crisis.

Capt. Thomas Bell and another fourteen members of the ship's crew perished. First mate James Thompson died when he went below to investigate the fire and was overcome by smoke. Another sailor, identified only as McAuley, fell overboard and drowned while trying to launch the aft lifeboat. The boat was swamped and sunk by a large wave. Twelve other men got away in the ship's forward lifeboat, but then died when the boat capsized in the storm.

The fire broke out somewhere below deck when the steamer was off Point Pelee, not far from the mouth of the Detroit River. The vessel was making what was to have been its last trip of the season, from Chicago to Buffalo, with a cargo of flour, corn and other items. Plans were to lay up at Erie for the winter.

Welch said the cause and the source of the fire were never known. He said he saw Thompson run below moments after the fire alarm was sounded. Thompson never returned. "He must have been overcome by the smoke which soon began to roll out of the hatchways in dense volumes. The fire spread so quickly that there was no time to effect a rescue. In

**Six crew members escaped when the *Clarion* burned in the midst of a Lake Erie gale.**

an incredibly short time the hold was a seething mass of flames and the boat, owing to the loss of her steering, was completely out of hand. We saw Captain Bell and the forward crew launching the big metallic lifeboat and we turned to the light wooden boat on the davits aft. Her lines were coated with ice, and long before we got them clear Captain Bell and the other members of the crew succeeded in getting away."

After the unsuccessful launch of the aft lifeboat and McAuley's fatal plunge into the sea, Welch said the men still aboard the burning ship found themselves in a desperate situation. "There we were, with a roaring furnace beneath our feet and without a boat, even if one could live in such a sea," he said.

Needless to say, the *Hanna* was a most welcome sight when it drew alongside the burning freighter.

The *Clarion* burned until it sank somewhere off Southeast Shoal.

# Wreck of the *Goodyear*

The ore carrier *Frank H. Goodyear* was the flagship of the Buffalo Steamship Company fleet. Named for the man who developed the famous Pullman railroad car, the *Goodyear* was distinguished by an ornate Pullman car attached to her deck. That railroad car, complete with a grand piano and fine furnishings, went to the bottom of lake Huron with the *Goodyear* and seventeen terrified sailors after a collision in fog with the freighter *James B. Wood* off Point aux Barques on the morning of May 23, 1910.

The *Goodyear* was downbound on Lake Huron with her holds stuffed with iron ore, steaming for her home port of Cleveland. It was about time for a change in the morning watch, so the cooks, Frank H. Bassett and his wife, Lillian, of Algonac, were busy fixing a hearty breakfast for the crew. Their three-year-old son, John, was with them in the mess hall nearby. The Bassetts sounded the call to breakfast at 5:45 AM and many of the workers were gathered in the mess when they heard a ship's whistle very close by. Almost instantly the four hundred and sixteen-foot long freighter gave such a violent lurch that many of the sailors were knocked off their feet. The *Wood's* bow had sliced hard into the side of the *Goodyear* at about amidships.

The first reaction was a wrong one. Everybody ran out on the deck to see what happened. Nobody realized how little time they had to save themselves. The *Goodyear* was nearly cut in two and was already starting its fall to the bottom of Lake Huron while people stood, gawking at the *Wood's* crushed bow looming overhead.

Bassett, perhaps prompted by the fact that he had his family on board, took immediate steps to save his wife and son. He put life preservers on everybody. About the time he was doing this, Basset said the boat jerked under him and something struck him in the back of the head, knocking him out. He woke up floating in the water, one of only five survivors.

Seventeen people died when the *Frank H. Goodyear* sank in a collision on Lake Huron. The boat was marked by an ornate Pullman
railroad car attached to the deck.

Another survivor was Frank's mother, Emma Basset,
the boat's porter. She said she was scrubbing the cabin floors
when she heard the whistles of both ships begin to blow. "The
fact that we were so close attracted my attention, and I went
on deck. A moment later the crash came and I grabbed one of
the life preservers." Mrs. Bassett said she slung the preserver
crudely over one arm and jumped over the rail and into the
water. She went under for a long time, then came back to the
surface, only to sink again. Finally she came to the top again
and managed to hang onto some floating debris until a yawl
boat from the *Wood* arrived to pull her out of the water. "It
was awful . . . while I was probably in the water for but a few
minutes, it seemed like hours," she said.

A member of the *Wood's* crew said he watched the sinking from the deck of his ship. It was a scene he probably carried to his grave. "Standing amidships on the *Goodyear* were
the entire crew, all huddled together, and I could see first one
and then another jump overboard. But suddenly the *Goodyear*
made a lurch to one side and went down out of sight, leaving
a big hole in the water. The suction carried the crew down
with it. The next I saw was a woman come to the top with a
child in her arms. One of the hatches then bubbled up and
struck her. I was forced to turn my head from the sickening

sight," the sailor said. That woman and child, undoubtedly Lillian and John Bassett, were killed by the crushing blow of the big wooden hatch cover as it rose up from under them.

Other witnesses said that the air pressure from the inrushing water blew some of the hatch covers high in the air moments before the *Goodyear* sank. They felt other crew members may have been killed as the covers fell back into the water on top of them.

The other survivors included fireman Frank Mollick of Chicago, and engineer George Grant, Carsonville, Michigan, who both ran from the engine room after the crash and jumped overboard; and Capt. F. R. Hemenger, Algonac. Hemenger declined comment about the wreck and about his personal experience.

Captain Gibson, master of the *Wood,* said he was too upset to tell his story. He ordered lifeboats lowered and his men spent about seven hours searching the area for survivors before he turned the *Wood* back to Port Huron.

The steamer *William Siemens,* commanded by Capt. William McElroy, arrived on the scene shortly after the sinking, and stood by for several hours. McElroy said he heard the whistles of the two boats and then the crash from about a mile away.

The *Goodyear* has never been found. It is believed to be in about two hundred forty feet of water, several miles off shore.

# The Unexplained Loss of *Pere Marquette 18*

The sinking of the railroad car ferry *Pere Marquette No. 18* on September 9, 1910, remains one of Lake Michigan's unsolved mysteries. The ship took twenty-nine passengers and crew to the bottom with her, then caused the deaths of two sailors from another vessel who fell from an overturned life-boat and drowned. Another thirty-three of the sixty-two persons aboard the doomed ferry were pulled from the water alive.

Nobody could explain why the ferry sank. There was no storm although seas were running high. The ship was not overloaded. Her engines and machinery were working. The vessel was making a first run in the ferry service after spending the summer as an excursion liner between Chicago and Waukegan. She had passed a government inspection at Ludington just the day before it was lost.

Why, then, did *Pere Marquette No. 18* sink?

Capt. Peter Kilty of Ludington probably knew what sank his boat, as did many of the officers. But Kilty and the officers were all killed. The survivors were unable to explain what happened.

There was a theory that some of the plates on the hull were damaged during the summer months while the steamer was serving as an excursion liner. After taking on ballast and twenty-nine rail cars, the ferry was riding low enough in the water that the damaged hull leaked. Another theory was that a sea cock was accidentally left open during the conversion from passenger to ferry service.

The ship was discovered taking on water at about 3:00 AM when it was about half way across Lake Michigan, on a run from Ludington to Milwaukee. A wheelsman in the pilot house complained that the ship was not steering well. At about the same time an oiler, who went aft from the engine room to oil the propeller shaft bearings, discovered seven feet of water in the stern.

Coal passer Thomas Shields said he was first aware of trouble when he saw water pouring into the ship through a porthole. "I saw the mate, Joe Brezenski, and one of the

**The sinking of *Pere Marquette No. 18* and the deaths of thirty-one people in 1910 remains one of Lake Michigan's great mysteries.**

wheelsmen come and try to fix the glass and the brass that holds the port in. Then Captain Kilty comes, and they push clothes and rags into the hole, and the captain orders the pumps to be put on. Then Captain Kilty tells us we've got to shove the cars off so as to lighten the ship," Shields said. He said he and other crew members pushed all twenty-nine railroad cars overboard that night.

Kilty ordered his ship headed due west at full steam, hoping to hit shoal water near Sheboygan. He also directed wireless operator S. F. Sczepanek to send what is believed to have been the first ship-to-shore radio distress signal in history. The international "S.O.S." code was not adopted in 1910, so Sczepanek sent: "C.Q.D., for God's sake, send help." A similar message was sent from the *Titanic* on the North Atlantic two years later.

Company officers at Ludington picked up the signal and sent *Pere Marquette No. 17,* which was steaming from Milwaukee to Ludington, to the scene. Her master, Captain Russell, said Kilty asked him to stand by when his ship arrived. Russell also found that *No. 18* was still underway, which made it difficult for his ship to pull alongside. Russell later was criticized for not pulling his boat alongside the sinking ship. Shields and a porter, Stanley Chubb, both said they thought everyone could have been saved if he had. While Kilty may have had visions of saving *No. 18,* there is evidence that the crew members knew their ship was sinking. Shields and Chubb said they heard second mate W. H. Brown ask *No. 17* to come alongside just minutes before the ship went down. They said he shouted "For God's sake, what are you doing?"

Shields said the men were ordered to drop the port side lifeboats, which were on the lee side of the ship, although they were not put all the way into the water. Some of the deck hands got in and kept them from banging on the side of the ship. "We loosened all the life rafts so they would float off when the boat sank," Shields added.

Russell said he was maneuvering *No. 17* around to the lee side of the stricken steamer so he would be in position to take people aboard when *No. 18* sank without warning. He said the bow rose high in the air and the ship slid stern first into the sea. As it went down, air pressure building in the bow caused the hull to explode. The explosion may have killed many of the people still on the boat.

Seymour E. Cochrane, who was on the ship with a crew of scrubbers and carpet layers to remodel some of the staterooms, said he had time to tie a purse with a thousand dollars in gold coins to the rail. He floated on a cabin door until he was rescued by lifeboats from *No. 17.*

The dead included Kilty, Brezenski of Manitowoc; Brown of Ludington; Sczepanek of Worcester, Massachusetts; chief engineer E. R. Leedham of Ludington; assistant engineer Chalmer Rosencranz of Northport, Michigan; second assistant engineer Paul Rennere of Ludington; passenger N. L. Bertrand of Ludington; fireman Michael Haythaler of Forestville, Michigan; fireman W. Parker of Marine City, Michigan; cabin maid Mrs. Marion Turner of Ludington; watchman Peter Hire of Ludington; wheelsman Ole Bakken of Ludington; scrubber Joseph Marion of Ludington; oiler Charles Jensen of Ludington; and two stowaways, Tom Kelley and an unnamed brother, both from Detroit.

Watchman Joe Peterson and scrubber Jacob Jacobson, crew members from Pere Marquette *No. 17,* drowned when their boat accidentally smashed against the side of the steamer and they tumbled into the lake.

The wreck lies about twenty miles off Sheboygan.

# Jinx Ship

When fire claimed the steamship *Maine* on the St. Clair River the night of July 16, 1911, it spelled the end of one of the most unlucky ships to ever sail the Great Lakes. Sailors may have called it a jinx or hoodoo ship because of the disasters that plagued its forty-nine-year career.

Despite three fires, a sinking and one boiler explosion, the *Maine* continued to rise up like a Phoenix from the ashes to sail again, until the fire at Marine City. The *Maine* was not a large vessel, although it was originally designed for both passenger and freight service. When launched at Cleveland in 1862, the boat measured a modest one hundred thirty-five feet and had a gross tonnage of slightly over four hundred.

The first disaster happened on July 5, 1871, as the steamer approached Ogdensburg, New York, on the St. Lawrence River, after a long trip down the lakes from Chicago. The *Maine* was only a mile from Ogdensburg when the boiler exploded, killing six people and wounding two.

The following summer the ship hit a rock in the Welland Canal developed a leak and sank in shallow water at Goose Bay, Lake Ontario. It was raised ten days later, repaired and returned to service.

The fires started at Port Huron on May 22, 1880. The *Maine* was tied up at the Northern Transit Company wharf when fire broke out in a cargo of jute in the hold at about 2:15 AM. The fire forced the crew to flee. The burning ship was set adrift in the St. Clair River to keep the flames from spreading to the dock and an adjoining warehouse. The propeller *Milwaukee*, docked nearby, cast off and steamed out into the river to escape the fire. The *Maine* drifted until it went aground on the Canadian side of the river and sank. The hull was raised a month later and the boat was rebuilt as a lumber carrier.

The *Maine* burned a second time on April 15, 1898, while fitting out at Tonawanda, New York. It was raised again and the scorched hull towed to Bay City, where the ship was rebuilt and returned to service in October, 1899.

**The *Maine* was a hard luck ship. It experienced three fires, a sinking and boiler explosion between the time it was built in 1862 until the day it burned for the last time in 1911.**

The boat served the lakes for another eleven years before a third fire finished it off in 1911. The steamer was under command of Capt. William Booth, steaming up the St. Clair River with a cargo of coal, when flames were discovered in the hold at 10:30 PM. The fire spread so quickly through the ship's wooden decks that Booth drove the vessel aground on the Canadian side of the river. The crew fled to shore, not taking time to collect personal clothing. This time the *Maine* burned to destruction.

# Lost Lumber Hooker

The *S. K. Martin* was typical of the lumber hookers of her day. A tired old wooden hulled ship that had seen better times as a busy passenger hauler between Chicago and other Lake Michigan ports, the *Martin,* now in her twenty-ninth year, was suffering from age. On the decks could be found a little dry rot, her engines were worn, and at a hundred and fifty-two feet, she wasn't large enough or fast enough to compete as an ore and grain hauler between Chicago to Buffalo.

The lumber companies were hard up for boats. They weren't fussy, so they were using anything that would float to carry the thousands of feet of prime hard and softwood trees to market from the forests of Michigan and Wisconsin. The *Martin,* under command of Capt. W. J. Jock, Mount Clemens, Michigan, found lots of work carrying lumber for Sicken's Mill at Marine City, to Buffalo. The ship was loaded with coal for the trip back up the lakes when a storm claimed it on Lake Erie on October 12, 1912.

The lumber hooker *S. K. Martin* foundered in Lake Erie in 1912. The crew escaped in a life boat.

Jock had contracted to haul coal from Buffalo to a Lake Michigan port that fall. Plans were to stop at Erie to pick up the barge *Melvina*, which was also making the trip. The *Martin* never made Erie. While battling some heavy weather, the old ship's wooden hull opened up at about 11:00 PM and it dropped to the bottom two hours later, about four miles offshore.

The crew told of a frantic run toward shore that afternoon while the water was rising in the hold faster than the pumps could handle it. Jock's decision to abandon ship came none too soon. The lifeboat was launched with all eleven crew members aboard only minutes before the *Martin* sank by the bow. Lake Erie is shallow so the masts were still showing when the ship hit bottom. The crew reached shore about two hours later and walked to a farmer's home for shelter.

The *Martin* was originally the *City of Saint Joseph* when it was launched at Benton Harbor in 1883. It served as a passenger ship until 1887.

# Heroine on the *Hanna*

Even though it was counted among the nineteen ships that were sunk or wrecked during the Great Storm of 1913, the *Howard M. Hanna Jr.* and its crew of twenty-five turned out to be survivors.

Captain Hager and his chief engineer Mayberry, told how the seas, stirred by seventy-mile-per-hour winds, swept the entire four hundred and eighty-foot steel vessel with such force they carried away part of the aft cabin, smashed windows and tore the roof from the pilot house. The seas continually raised the rudder and propeller out of the water putting the ship out of control. The *Hanna* broached in the trough of the seas and her engines did not have enough power to bring the bow around into the wind again. The ship drifted out of control until the storm drove it on the rocks near Port Austin, Michigan.

Mayberry said he had the engines running at top speed, trying to help the captain keep the vessel turned into the gale. He said the pumps also were running at full blast as sailors tried to get the water out of the hold as fast as it was seeping in. "Everything went well until about six thirty (in the afternoon). Then the oiler's door was smashed in on the starboard side, and the two engine room doors went in and the windows. At that time, the water was rushing in the engine room," Mayberry said. He said that when the cabin area housing the kitchen and dining room got swept off the stern, part of the woodwork came crashing down the open doorway into the engine room. "The water kept coming in until we went on the beach at ten o'clock."

By the time the *Hanna* went on Port Austin Reef, the cabins were smashed and the stack was toppled. The ship later cracked in the middle, cutting electric power and communications from the engine room to the bow. Crew members were trapped for several hours at both ends of the wreck, without a way to talk to each other or keep warm. It was the ship's cook, a remarkable woman identified as Mrs. Clarence

Mrs. Black, the ship's cook, kept morale up and helped the crew of the *Howard M. Hanna Jr.* survive the Great Storm of 1913.

Black of Chicago, who kept morale up during the long hours that followed. They said she stood in water up to her waist, and exposed herself to the storm to keep a fire burning in the galley stove in her wrecked kitchen. Hot coffee was served from Sunday night until Tuesday morning when lifesavers reached the ship.

Black later was hospitalized at Port Huron for treatment of exposure and exhaustion. The crew took up a collection on her behalf. One sailor said she was a frail woman, weighing about a hundred pounds, and was making her final trip before retiring.

The *Hanna* was on its way from Lorain, Ohio, to Fort William, Ontario, with soft coal when the storm caught it off Pointe aux Barques.

The ship later was salvaged, rebuilt and returned to service as the Canadian steamer *Glenshee*. It later operated under the names *Marquette, Goderich, Agawa* and finally as a grain storage barge known as *Lionel Parsens* until 1983, when scrapped at Thunder Bay, Ontario.

# Saved from the *Choctaw*

Some sailors might have said the whaleback steamer *Choctaw* was jinxed. But that was a matter of personal judgment. The *Choctaw* claimed three lives when it blew a cylinder head on Lake St. Clair in 1893, a year after the boat was launched, but after that its record was clean.

When it met an untimely end in a collision with the Canadian freighter *Wahcondah* off Lake Huron's Presque Isle on July 12, 1915, all twenty members of the crew escaped. They got away, although there were some anxious moments.

Capt. Charles Fox said the two ships came together in thick fog about five miles off Presque Isle at 4:30 AM. The *Choctaw*, a Cleveland-Cliffs Iron Company vessel, was steaming north from Cleveland to Duluth with a cargo of coal, and the *Wahcondah* was downbound with grain for Montreal.

Fox said the *Wahcondah* came out of the gloom without warning and drove its bow deep into the port side of the *Choctaw*, between the number one and number two hatches. The men scrambled for lifeboats while the ship took an ominous list to port. Everybody was off the whaleback before it turned on its side and sank in two hundred feet of water about twenty minutes later.

The *Wahcondah's* bow was badly crushed, but the ship remained afloat. It picked up the *Choctaw's* crew and then limped slowly south to Sarnia, not arriving until the following day.

Most ships weren't yet equipped with radios in 1915, so the full story of the collision wasn't told until the *Wahcondah* reached Sarnia and the crew of the *Choctaw* came across the St. Clair River to Port Huron. But the word reached Port Huron ahead of the sailors that something terrible had happened to the *Choctaw*.

Capt. Nelson Brown, master of the steamer *James H. Reed,* discovered wreckage with the name *Choctaw* on it a few hours after the ship went down. Brown reported what he found when the *Reed* arrived at Sault Ste. Marie later in the day, and the story spread via the telegraph wires along the coast. For a few hours it was feared that Fox and his entire crew were lost. The news of their survival was most welcome.

Sailors who believe in hard-luck ships had to admit that the *Choctaw* wasn't so bad after all. It was lost, but it let the crew escape to sail again.

The *Choctaw* gave the crew time to escape when it was sunk in a collision on Lake Huron.

# The *Eastland* Horror

The very mention of the steamer *Eastland* still stirs black thoughts of hundreds of screaming men, women and children trapped below decks to drown aboard a capsized excursion liner.

Anyone who watched the Hollywood movie *The Poisidon Adventure,* about a liner overturned by a great tidal wave at sea, might have some idea what it might have been like for the twenty-four hundred passengers and seventy-two crew members aboard the *Eastland* on July 24, 1915 when the ship tipped on its side and sank in Chicago harbor. Of that number, eight hundred and thirty-five people perished. The disaster still ranks with the sinking of the *Titanic,* the torpedoing of the *Lusitania* and the burning of the steamer *General Slocom* off New York's Hell Gate as the worst of all marine tragedies. No other single accident on the Great Lakes claimed as many lives.

The *Eastland* was one of five liners chartered that fateful morning to take an estimated seven thousand employees of the Western Electric Company on a day-long picnic excursion to Michigan City, Indiana. The tickets sold for seventy-five cents and children got aboard without charge. First arrivals at the dock boarded the *Eastland* which was scheduled to be the first of the vessels to leave. When officials decided the *Eastland* was filled to capacity, they began directing passengers over the Clark Street bridge to the steamer *Theodore Roosevelt.* Also docked to take passengers were the steamers *Petoskey, Racine* and *Maywood.*

*Chicago Herald* reporter Harlan E. Babcock was among the crowds still waiting on the dock. He said he noticed even before it tipped that the *Eastland* seemed to be listing from the weight of so many people on her upper decks. "I vaguely remembered having heard that the *Eastland* had been condemned some years ago and I felt that the crew was taking awful chances in overcrowding the boat, especially as the vessel kept listing gradually but more and more every minute

Death scene on the Chicago River after the *Eastland* capsized. Eight
hundred and thirty-five people died.

toward the river. Then a tugboat steamed alongside and gave
several deep-throated blasts, which evidently was the signal
to 'cast off' and start. But it never cast off. Before even the
crew had time to release the hawsers that held the boat to the
dock, the vessel began to topple, and in less time than it takes
to tell it, the sight of that horror stricken throng of thousands,
the *Eastland* . . . careened, hurling hundreds screaming into
the black waters of the river."

A story in that day's *Herald* described the events that
followed: "There was a mad scramble, a panic in which the
terrified passengers fought for places of safety. Shrieks and
cries wrung the hearts of those on shore. A minute or two
more and the ship was flat on its side . . . and those caught
beneath and within were entombed . . . The surface of the
river was thick with struggling forms. Babies perished in sight
of those on the docks and bridges. The witnesses say it was
all over in between four and six minutes."

The nearby streets and warehouses, and the steamer
*Theodore Roosevelt* were turned that day into morgues. As
they were pulled from the water, and as workers cut others
from the ship, the bodies were piled in rows. Ambulances,

vans and trucks were pressed into service as death carts. It was a tragic scene that will remain fixed in the bleaker moments of Chicago's past.

The exact cause of the disaster has always remained a mystery. After months of hearings, authorities officially blamed an obscure engineer who they said neglected to properly fill the ship's ballast tanks. Other theories ranged from an overloaded ship that was resting on a sloping river bottom, to a sudden rush of passengers to the port side to view a passing launch. Still others blamed a tug, which they said was pulling on the *Eastland* before her lines were released from the dock.

The ballast tanks may, indeed, have played a key part in the disaster. To understand why we must look at the *Eastland's* history and events leading up to the Chicago disaster.

When the ship was launched at Port Huron, Michigan, on May 6, 1903, the Jenks Shipbuilding Company and the entire town treated it as a major event. Mrs. J. C. Perue, wife of the ship's first captain, broke a bottle of champagne over her bow. Mrs. Deila Reid of South Haven, Michigan, who won a contest to name the *Eastland*, was presented a check for ten dollars and a pass for a free trip. As the hull rumbled down the ways and hit the water in the Black River, whistles sounded and people cheered. She was the first passenger boat built in Port Huron in twenty years. The newspapers were filled with praises and graphic descriptions of the ship's stylish dining rooms, staterooms and other fine points.

A story in the *Port Huron Times Herald* also noted that "the bottom is double, there being a space of four feet between the lower and upper bottom . . . the space being divided into ten water compartments used for water ballast, allowing the ship's draft to vary from ten feet to sixteen feet in a short space of time." This feature was not uncommon in lake vessels. While many ships of the day used water tanks for ballast, none were designed quite like the *Eastland*. Each of the compartments could be individually pumped out or filled at the discretion of the captain and crew.

Speculation about why the *Eastland's* ballast tanks existed in this way was varied. One story was that the ship needed to blow her ballast to clear the sand bars at the entrance to various ports on the Great Lakes. Another theory was that the gangways, or side loading doors, were built so low in the side of the ship that the water ballast had to be pumped out when the *Eastland* was in port to bring the gangways level with the loading docks. A Chicago newspaper reported that the *Eastland's* crew did that very thing on the day of the disaster.

Why did Signey G. Jenks, the man who designed the *Eastland,* engineer a ship that had to be raised and lowered each time she made port? The answer may lie in the contract Jenks made with the *Eastland's* first owners, the Michigan Transportation Company.

Competition was fierce among steamboat lines for the passenger and excursion trade at the turn of the century, and the company wanted a fast passenger ship to compete for business between Chicago and South Haven. In fact, the contract called for guarantees that this boat would travel at a speed of twenty miles an hour for at least four consecutive hours. If the ship failed to make this speed, the contract contained a penalty clause costing the builders twenty-five hundred dollars for every quarter mile per hour the *Eastland* fell short of the goal. If the speed fell short by a full mile per hour, the builders agreed to forfeit ten thousand dollars from the two hundred and thirty-five thousand dollar contract price.

In other words, Jenks designed the *Eastland* for speed. While it was two hundred sixty-five feet long, he made the steel hull only thirty-eight feet, two inches wide. This made the ship about two feet thinner than the sleekest of ships then traveling the lakes. Jenks also installed two thirty-five hundred horse triple expansion engines that drove the boat's twin propellers.

Even after all of this care in planning, Jenks was horrified when the *Eastland* failed to get up to the mandated twenty-mile-per-hour speed during her trial runs. The ship went back to the dry dock and modifications were made, which Jenks only described as "a forced draft." Modern-day experiments with hull design have proved that when boat hulls are lifted higher in the water, resistance is reduced and speed can be increased. While there is nothing on record to prove it, Jenks' so-called "forced draft" may have been the installation of pumps to get the water in and out of the ballast tanks on demand. Taking the water out of the ballast tanks while underway would make the ship ride higher, create less resistance, and allow the boat to meet the speed requirements in the contract.

Jenks may also have removed the ship's keel.

In spite of his modifications, Jenks always maintained that the *Eastland* was a safe ship. "She was seaworthy in every respect," he said. Her forty-three-year history of service would appear to support his claim. Prior to the Chicago tragedy, the ship carried thousands of passengers between 1903 and 1915 without a serious accident. After it tipped over, the Navy bought the hull, removed the high superstructure, and turned it into the training ship *Wilmette*. The *Wilmette* sailed the lakes until the Navy scrapped it in 1946.

Yet while she was sailing as the *Eastland,* rumors persisted that it was a dangerous ship. Sailors labeled her as a "cranky" and "hoodoo" ship almost from the day she was put on the Chicago to South Haven run. John Adams, chief engineer on the rival steamer *City of South Haven,* said he remembered a time in 1906 when the *Eastland* nearly capsized with a full load of passengers in the middle of Lake Michigan. Adams said his ship was steaming just behind the *Eastland* when a cold wind suddenly developed out of the north and

The steamer *Eastland* entering the harbor at South Haven, Michigan.

deck passengers all moved to the lee side of the boat. "We saw her suddenly list to one side," he said. "The *Eastland* reduced its speed and after about a half hour she was again righted. We . . . expected to see her capsize at any moment and it seemed to me nothing short of a miracle that she did not."

That incident caused federal authorities to take a second look at the *Eastland*, and they soon started putting restrictions on her passenger loads.

The *Eastland* was sold the following year to the Lake Shore Navigation Company, and later the Eastland Navigation Company, both at Cleveland. She was put on a run between Cleveland and Cedar Point. Here, the vessel again gained a reputation of being top heavy, unwieldy and unsafe.

To fight the rumors, her owners tore out upper staterooms and added heavy ballast, and for awhile ran a heavy advertising campaign proclaiming the ship's safety record. Government inspectors were still concerned. During that period, the *Eastland* was licensed to carry no more than six hundred and fifty-three passengers. Because she didn't carry enough lifeboats to accommodate them, the ship was required to stay within five miles of land, and in waters shallow enough that if it sank, the *Eastland* would not be fully submerged.

Strangely enough, when the *Eastland* was bought by the Chicago-St. Joseph Steamship Company and brought back to Chicago in the spring of 1915 for the excursion trade, she was re-licensed to carry twenty-five hundred passengers. The new owners also did some extensive remodeling, adding more upper deck space. Some stories suggested that extra ballast added at Cleveland was removed and the ship lightened again so she could get in and out of the Chicago River.

There were hints that government inspectors were either bribed, or in some other way persuaded to allow for the increased passenger loads for the sake of big profits. A story in the *Chicago Herald* quoted Illinois Attorney Maclay Hoyne as saying that members of the United States Inspection Bureau were aware that the *Eastland* was unsafe, but they licensed her to carry big passenger loads anyway. "If the inspectors of the bureau had done their duty, the accident could not have occurred. We know the ship was considered unsafe by them, because there are letters on file in Washington which predicted Saturday's occurrence. I have copies of these letters," Hoyne said. John D. York, an expert on naval design, wrote one of those letters. York told a coroner's jury after the disaster that he wrote the U. S. harbor inspector in 1913 to complain that he believed the *Eastland* was unseaworthy and dangerous. "It had no keel," he said. "She is a thirty-eight-beam boat and should have a forty-inch keel. The *Eastland* was never fit for navigable waters. She had a government license which should never have been granted her. The inspectors should never have passed her hull at any time, even for quiet stream navigation, not to speak of the big lake and river transits."

An Illinois grand jury leveled indictments charging negligence and manslaughter against Capt. Harry Pedersen, chief engineer Joseph M. Erickson, two steamboat inspectors and an official of the Indiana Transportation Company. But a federal judge rejected the petitions for lack of sufficient evidence. Hundreds of law suits were filed, but no one ever collected. A Circuit Court of Appeals in Chicago upheld a lower court ruling in 1935, twenty years after the disaster, that the St. Joseph-Chicago Steamship Company was not liable for the deaths.

# Two Survivors

Second mate Joseph Mudra and fireman Otto Lindquist lived to tell how the steamer *S. R. Kirby* broke up and sank during a Lake Superior gale on May 8, 1916. Other than the ship's mascot, a bulldog named Tige, they were the only ones among a crew of twenty-one sailors to survive the wreck. Both men said they got away because they were on deck when the ship unexpectedly cracked in two and plunged to the bottom at about 10:50 AM.

The *Kirby* was beating its way down the lakes from Ashland, Wisconsin, with a load of iron ore bound for Cleveland. Mudra said he was standing the morning watch as the ship battled a sixty-mile-per-hour gale off Eagle Harbor. He said he heard a loud crack that "sounded as though a heavy sea had hit the ship. When I looked around I saw number one hatch crumpling up and then, without a bit of warning, the ship began to buckle." He said the *Kirby* sank so fast most of

The *S. R. Kirby* sank on Lake Superior when it broke in two during a storm in 1916. There were only two survivors.

the men were trapped at their jobs below deck or else they were caught asleep in the forecastle. After he was tossed in the water, Madra managed to get on a raft which broke loose from the ship. He was picked up by the steamer *H. A. Berwind* about an hour later.

Lindquist said he had just stepped out of his cabin in the stern in time to be on deck when the steamer buckled. He said he dove head-first into the sea and then held onto a piece of wreckage until he was picked up by the steamer *Joseph Block* about the same time Mudra was rescued. Lindquist said he saw Capt. David Girardin Jr. swimming nearby in the water, but that Girardin later sank out of sight. The dog was rescued by the Coast Guard from a piece of wreckage three days later.

The barge *George E. Hartnell,* which was being towed by the *Kirby,* broke loose in the storm. There were fears that the seven sailors aboard it also were lost. The steamer *E. H. Utley* came on the drifting barge and towed it to safety.

The *Kirby* was a composite ship made of wood and steel. She was built at Wyandotte in 1890.

# The Ship That Toppled a Water Tower

The *Christopher Columbus* was one of the most popular and successful passenger liners ever to travel the Great Lakes. That was odd because the *Columbus* was a strange appearing ship. It had a passenger liner superstructure mounted on a whaleback hull, making it the only whaleback passenger vessel ever built.

Somehow, people liked the ugly looking ship with the bow that looked like the snout of a pig. Those who booked passage said it offered a smooth ride, even in a rolling sea, and it boasted an almost perfect safety record.

Almost.

There was one serious accident that marred her forty-four-year career. It happened at Milwaukee on June 30, 1917, when the ship accidentally struck and toppled a hundred-foot tall water tower at the edge of the Milwaukee River.

The tower crashed into the side of the bridge and dropped through three decks, flooding the ship. Sixteen passengers were killed and another thirty people were injured in the freak accident. It could have been worse. There were more than five hundred passengers aboard, most of them students and teachers from Northwestern University, the University of Chicago and other summer schools in Chicago.

The three hundred sixty-two-foot-long Goodrich Line steamer brought them to Milwaukee earlier that day and was just pulling out of the river for the second half of a day-long excursion. Passengers crowded the upper decks forward to watch as tugs worked the steamer backward down the river to a basin near the East Water Street Bridge, and then began turning it around for the trip out into Lake Michigan.

It was standard procedure, but this time, something went wrong. A strong river current was blamed. The bow of the ship was driven into the east bank of the river where it struck one leg of the water tower. Passengers stood in terror as the tower quivered and the steel framework began to buckle. Then the tank, filled with tons of water, dropped on top of them.

The *Chrisopher Columbus* was the only passenger liner built on a whaleback style hull. It had an almost perfect safety record.

Capt. Charles E. Moody was on the bridge and saw the impending danger. He ordered the ship's engines operating full astern moments before the tower fell. The *Christopher Columbus* was beginning to back away when the tank came down. Moody and wheelsman James Brody miraculously escaped injury even though the pilot house and wheel house below, where they stood, were demolished. "The next thing I knew the pilot house was lying all around me and Brody was nowhere to be seen. I must have been stunned," Moody later recalled. "I called, 'Jim, Jim,' as loud as I could, then I heard him call back: 'Here, captain.' I crawled over the deck where he was, about ten feet, and there he sat, crying."

All around them was devastation. The decks were ripped into kindling and many people were found crushed to pulp beneath the weight of wood and iron. Other passengers were knocked off the decks, and still others were believed to have jumped or fallen into the river to drown. Witnesses said the dining salon of the *Columbus* was like a slaughter house. Those not hit by the crushing force of the tank and collapsing decks, were deluged with twenty-five thousand gallons of water. Staterooms were awash. Some passengers were said to have jumped when they saw the rush of water coming at them across the decks.

As serious as the accident was, the *Christopher Columbus* went on sailing the lakes for another nineteen years before it was scrapped at Manitowoc, Wisconsin, in 1936.

# The Sinking Sandsucker

The sandsuckers on the Great Lakes today are probably all owned and operated by the Army Corps of Engineers and used for keeping harbors and navigable rivers open for vessels to pass. In earlier times, before the world was thinking about pollution and the ugly chemicals that might be lying down there, private companies made a business of extracting sand from the bottom of the lakes and selling it.

That was the business of the wooden hulled propeller *Desmond* during the last eight years she served the lakes. Owned by the Cream City Sand Company, of Milwaukee, the *Desmond* saw an active life, generally working from harbor-to-harbor along the Lake Michigan coast.

The boat was completing one of its last planned trips of the season when it sprang a leak and sank in a bad winter gale off South Chicago Lighthouse on December 8, 1917. Seven sailors died, but six others were saved when Chicago harbor tugs pulled them from the water at the last moment.

The *Desmond,* under the command of Capt. Emil Thorsen, left St. Joseph in southwestern Lower Michigan in the afternoon bound northwest for Racine, Wisconsin, with a load of sand. The boat was blown off course, however, when caught in a storm that brought high winds and sub-zero degree temperatures out of the north. The storm was so terrible Thorsen decided to try to make Chicago harbor instead of continuing a course against the wind and seas.

Survivor Herman Lederhaus said crew members feared for their lives and pleaded with Thorsen to run the ship on the beach someplace. Thorsen refused. "In thirty years on the lakes, I never have lost a ship. If the *Desmond* goes down, I will go with her," he answered. Thorsen died with his ship that day. The tragedy is that he almost made it.

The rolling seas shifted the sand in the *Desmond's* hold, causing a dangerous list to starboard. Crew members shoveled desperately, trying to get the vessel back on an even keel. The lights of Chicago harbor were in sight when the ship developed a serious leak in the stern at about 2:00 AM. Chief engineer Jack Stahl was forced to shut down the engines and use all the available steam pressure to operate the ship's pumps. Still the water gained.

The crew worked desperately for the rest of the night, trying to keep their ship afloat and hoping that someone on shore would notice their plight and send help. The water continued to rise until one of the coal bunkers collapsed. Floating pieces of coal clogged the pumps and siphons. The ship's list grew worse and it looked as if only a miracle would save it.

Thorsen made one final attempt to keep the Desmond afloat. Lederhaus told how Thorsen and four others launched a lifeboat. They apparently planned to row into the harbor and bring back a tugboat. As the little boat started away, the ship suddenly lurched and tipped on its side. The stack hit and capsized the lifeboat, causing all five sailors to tumble in the water.

Lederhaus said he and seven other men on the *Desmond* scrambled over the side as the ship rolled. He said

The master of the *Desmond* perished trying to save his ship when it got caught in a storm off Chicago.

the boat floated on its side for quite a while, while the men tried to ride out the storm on top of the overturned wreck. "I threw a rope to the five who were struggling in the water. Two of them, the captain and (Frank) Kipper, seized it. We pulled them to the side of the ship. Captain Thorsen froze to death as he lay there.

"We shouted and screamed and waved our coats until we became too numb to move. Finally, we attracted the attention of men on board a steamer," Lederhaus said. That steamer was the tug *William A. Field,* under command of Capt. William Bowen. No sooner had the *Field* spotted the overturned *Desmond,* then two other tugs, the *Gary* and *North Harbor,* also were steaming to the rescue.

Lederhaus, first mate Arthur M. Emkey, second engineer T. J. Cunningham, Kipper, Carl Olson and Gus Yonson were all rescued alive before the ship sank at about 7:00 AM. Dead were Thorsen, Stahl, Fred Cuby, John Henning, Arthur Hibbard and two unidentified sailors known only as Louis and Pete.

# Part 4:
# Contemporary
# Calamities
# 1920 to 1975

# The Ship That Came Home to Die

Did the steamer *William H. Wolf* come home to die? The twenty-one surviving crew members probably had no doubt of it after their experience with the burning boat in the fall of 1921.

After thirty-four faithful years the tired old *Wolf,* which once boasted of being the largest vessel on the Great Lakes, seemed to know her days were numbered. The signs of trouble came quickly. The steamer had trouble weathering a September 18 gale on Lake Superior and sank at the entrance to Portage Waterway. She settled in shallow water so was pumped out and raised the next day. Capt. J. T. Hanson, Detroit, brought his ship into Houghton to unload the coal in her holds, and then took on a load of pulpwood. It was the last scheduled cargo for the season and was bound for Port Huron Sulfite and Paper Company. After that, plans were to run the boat to Detroit and lay it up for the winter.

The *Wolf* made the trip down the lakes without incident. She remained quietly docked while the crew unloaded the cargo. Then late on the night of October 19, Hanson told engineer M. E. Anderson, Detroit, to build up steam. The lines were cast off and the empty ship, its hull riding high, started down the St. Clair River for Detroit.

She never arrived. A fire of unknown cause was discovered in the forward crew's quarters just under the bridge at about 1:00 AM. Before the night was over, first mate Edward Henry of Detroit and wheelman Anthony Smith of Ashland, Wisconsin, were dead. Hanson was hospitalized with burns and a fractured leg, and the *Wolf* was a smoking ruin aground on Fawn Island, near Marine City. It was almost as if the old ship waited until her work was finished and she had delivered her crew as close as possible to their home ports of Port Huron and Detroit before she went up in flames.

The fire broke out an hour after the change of watch, when most of the boat's crew was asleep. Second Mate Edward Taylor of Port Huron became a hero of the hour for di-

Two men were killed when the *William H. Wolf* burned on the St. Clair River in 1921.

recting rescue operations. He later told how the sailors were roused from their sleep and then led out into the night to fight the blaze. He said fire fighters were hampered by a stiff wind that fanned the aggressive flames throughout the ship's wooden decks and superstructure. The mate, who lead the fire fighting efforts at first, climbed into the forward hold to check the extent of the fire there. He was overcome with smoke and never returned. The sailors said Smith lost his head and jumped overboard. He perished in the water.

Hanson knew his command was doomed so he drove the ship aground on Fawn Island while there was still steam up. There were two reasons: It would gave the crew a chance to escape and it got the burning ship out of the busy shipping lane. His decision became an epic of personal heroism. Hanson ordered everyone out of the pilot house and then stood alone at the wheel, with fire burning below and all around him, until the *Wolf* hit bottom. It was a long and fearful trip. By the time the boat was grounded, it was too late for Hanson to flee to the stern with the others. He had no choice but to make a dash through the flames to the rail and lower himself over the side. Here, with his face burned and his hair singed, he found the anchor chain and wrapped himself around it, waiting for help.

Marine City resident John Marquette was on the way. He was among the first to see the fire from shore and he took his personal power boat out on the river to help. When he saw Hanson clinging to the ship's chain, he called to him to jump. Hanson heard and tried to drop into the water, but his foot was still tangled in the chain and the fall fractured his leg in two places. Marquette pulled him from the water and then took him to Marine City for medical help.

In the meantime, Taylor found himself in command of the stern of the burning boat. He had the ship's lifeboat lowered and then brought the crew to shore in two separate trips. The first load went to the Canadian side, which was closer. The final boat load went to Marine City on the Michigan side.

Among the men brought safely off the *Wolf* were B. Ferwerdan, J. A. Johnson, Robert Lee, E. A. Slove, Paul Ailiguin, W. Waliburg and K. Termeria, all of Detroit; Thomas Cosgrove, William Gilmartin, James Flanning, W. T. Walsh, Arthur and William Tacle, Harry Cascadden, Earl McNiece, Walter Wright, William Pettee and Harvey Jones, all of Port Huron.

# The Miracle of the *Conger* Explosion

The horror of the blast that wrecked the ferry *Omar D. Conger* and sent four sailors off to eternity on March 26, 1922, caused people at first to overlook the fact that a miracle had happened.

The explosion sent pieces of the red-hot boiler flying hundreds of feet through the air in all directions where they left a path of destruction. A two hundred-pound radiator fell through the roof of the Falk Undertaking Parlors where mourners were gathered for a funeral, part of the boiler demolished a nearby house, and a second steamship with about two hundred passengers was only a few hundred feet away and approaching the dock. While others were hurt, the miracle was that only four people died.

The steamer *Cheboygan* was within two hundred feet of the *Conger,* and was approaching the dock next to the ill-fated ship when the explosion rocked the waterfront at 2:20 PM. Nobody aboard the *Cheboygan* was hurt. Had the ship been closer, or docked, a number more people could have been seriously hurt or killed.

Capt. George W. Waugn was standing on the bridge of the *Cheboygan* and saw what happened. "I heard the explosion and looked up and saw a cloud of smoke and dust where the *Conger* had been. I was deafened and sort of dazed for a few seconds and the next thing I saw her hull was sinking and debris was scattered all around. The boat sunk almost in an instant. It looked as though the explosion blew the boiler right through the side of the hull," Waugn said.

The William Smith family was not at home when the piece of the boiler crashed down on their house. They were trying out a newly purchased car and Smith got it stuck in the mud. While he was perhaps cursing his ill fortune, he was unaware that the delay in returning home was saving his life and the lives of his family. Not only was the house destroyed, but the heat from the boiler caused the debris to burn. Every thing the Smiths owned was lost.

**Four people died when the ferry *Omar D. Conger* blew up at Port Huron, Michigan.**

When the radiator came through the roof at Falk Undertaking Parlor, flying glass and pieces of the roof left several mourners hurt and very frightened. Some were trampled in the panic that followed.

Two crew members who should have been aboard the *Conger* that afternoon, were delayed and thus were saved. Capt. William P. Major was in close proximity. He was walking toward the boat and was in front of the Falk Undertaking Parlor. He saw the heavy radiator fall through the roof. Shirley R. Busby, an assistant engineer, was late boarding the ferry because he missed the trolley from his home.

The *Conger* was scheduled to sail for Sarnia at 3:00 PM and some passengers had already arrived at the dock. But none of the passengers had yet boarded the ship. The four crew members who died were on board, firing up the boiler and getting the *Conger* ready for the day's first trip across the St. Clair River. They were engineer Ransome A. Campbell, fireman Clifford D. Althouse, and deck hands Thomas Buckner and Kenneth R. Crandall.

Investigation showed that the boiler was either out of water, or the water was very low when the fires were kindled. The blast occurred when someone opened a valve that let cold water pour into an overheated boiler.

The *Conger,* which bore the name of a U. S. Senator from Port Huron, was built at Port Huron only a few hundred feet from where it blew up. She was a small craft, only ninety-two feet in length, and was built to be the vessel she was. The *Conger* spent her forty years working faithfully as a ferry, carrying passengers between Port Huron and Sarnia, and making occasional excursions up and down the St. Clair River.

# Trapped on a Sinking Ship

The master of the Canadian freighter *Glenorchy* was proclaimed a hero, even though he lost his ship and a cargo valued at more than four hundred thousand dollars. That's because Capt. Fred Burke risked his own life when he stayed aboard his sinking boat to save a crew member trapped below deck.

It happened on October 29, 1924, when the *Glenorchy* collided with the *Leonard B. Miller* in dense fog on Lake Huron, about six miles southeast of Harbor Beach. The *Glenorchy* was downbound with grain in its hold when it entered a fog bank at about noon. Burke said he ordered the ship's speed reduced. When the fog got thicker, he slowed the boat to about three miles an hour. "Visibility was only a few yards and we were blowing the whistle." At about 2:00 PM, the crew heard the sound of a whistle on an approaching ship dead ahead. Burke said he ordered the *Glenorchy* turned to starboard to get clear of the other ship. The maneuver was a mistake. It put the freighter on a collision course with the *Miller*.

**The captain risked his life to save a trapped member of his crew when the *Glenorchy* sank in a collision on Lake Huron.**

"The bows of the *Miller* loomed up through the fog only about sixty or seventy feet away. It was impossible to avoid her," Burke said. "Her prow cut into us just aft of the port anchor and did not stop until her nose was clear up to the bridge." The crash threw watchman John Scott into a wall of the pilot house and first mate James McMillian was knocked off his feet to the deck. Scott was later treated for bruises and a bad case of nerves in a Sarnia hospital. McMillian was not hurt.

Burke said the *Glenorchy* started to list at once and "I knew she was going fast. We made ready to man the boats but it wasn't necessary because the *Miller* came alongside and took us aboard."

Burke didn't comment about what happened next, but newspaper clippings of the day made sure everybody knew. They said that when the captain learned that one crew member, Ward White, was trapped in a stateroom, he went back to get the man out. With his ship literally sinking under his feet, Burke used an ax to chop his way through a jammed stateroom door to reach White. It was a dramatic rescue. Moments after Burke and White stepped to the deck of the waiting *Miller,* the *Glenorchy* turned on its port side, then went bottom-up and sank.

The *Miller,* which had been upbound with a cargo of coal, took all twenty members of the *Glenorchy's* crew aboard, and then limped back to Port Huron, her bow pushed in, a large hole in her port side, and the pumps barely keeping ahead of the incoming water. The *Miller's* master, Capt. William Hagen, declined comment.

The *Glenorchy* lies upside down in about a hundred and twenty feet of water. She is well known to sport divers.

# Just Three Hundred Feet Short

Battered by fifteen foot waves and a fierce northeaster, the steamer *W. H. Sawyers's* luck ran out on August 11, 1928 as the boat dashed for the safety of the Harbor Beach breakwall. The *Sawyer* plunged to the bottom of Lake Huron, just three hundred feet from safety and within sight of the Harbor Beach Coast Guard station. The ship bubbled down to thirty feet of water so the two masts were visible above the surface for several days, marking the ship's grave and that of the boat's cook who went down with it.

The cook was John J. Buckley, a Detroit man who signed on a few days before the *Sawyer* sailed. He was so new the crew members didn't know his last name. Buckley apparently got seasick during the storm and was spending time in his bunk below as the ship battled the storm. He was still there when the boat sank. His body washed ashore a week later.

Sailing north with the barges *A. B. King* and *Peshtigo* in tow, the *Sawyer* was bound from Toledo for Lake Superior with salt. The barges were carrying either crushed limestone or salt. The *Sawyer* stalled for about a day on the St. Clair River under a thick fog, so Capt. August Galonbisky was pushing the thirty-eight-year-old boat through the storm to make up for lost time. He chose not to make an unscheduled stop at Harbor Beach that day, even though the storm was already turning into a serious gale at about the time the three vessels battled their way past that port.

It was later in the night when wind reached an estimated fifty miles an hour that Galonbisky had second thoughts. His ship was getting so battered by the storm that the ship's wooden hull was beginning to leak. When somewhere off Port Hope, Galonbisky turned around for a trip back to Harbor Beach. As the *Sawyer* turned, however, the tow line parted, sending the two barges adrift to battle the storm on their own. The *King,* a one hundred seventy-seven-foot vessel, was carrying a crew of six men and a woman cook.

The **W. H. Sawyer** got close, but failed to make Harbor Beach before it sank in 1928.

The other, the two hundred-foot *Peshtigo*, also had a crew of seven aboard. Both barges were blown on the rocks off Port Hope. Their crews were rescued the next day by life savers from nearby Pointe aux Barques.

Meanwhile, the *Sawyer* was steaming hard, with the wind at her stern, for shelter at Harbor Beach. Galonbisky raced against time. The water in the hold was mixing with the salt. The salt water was jamming the ship's pumps.

The boat almost made it. As the harbor loomed in sight, Coast Guard Commander Davidson watched the *Sawyer's* lights shortly before 3:00 AM. There was no radio aboard the ship, but Davidson knew from the way the vessel was taking the waves that it was in trouble. He assembled his life saving crew. The *Sawyer* sank so quickly that Galonbisky, his first mate and wheelsman floated off into the water from the pilot house. All three were picked up by life savers. Other crew members washed ashore, clinging to wreckage.

Wreckage from the *Sawyer* drifted ashore for miles along the coast. The ship had to be destroyed by dynamite because it was lying at the entrance to the harbor and was considered a hazard to other vessels.

The *Peshtigo* was the only one of the three vessels salvaged. The *King* also was destroyed in the storm.

# "Hope to God We're Saved!"

The gravel laden freighter *Andaste* might have been classified as a tramp steamer the day it sank with all hands in a Lake Michigan gale, somewhere off Holland, Michigan. Critics said the thirty-seven-year-old ship was suffering from lack of maintenance: her davits were so rusted the lifeboats could not be lowered, there was no electric power, and she was not equipped with radio, even though most vessels had ship-to-shore communications by 1929.

The ship was a strange vessel. At least her profile was unusual. She was a whaleback, one of about forty boats with cigar-shaped hulls designed by Scotsman Alexander McDougall before the turn of the century. A self-unloading system installed in 1921 was the final insult. People who knew the *Andaste* may even have thought of her as a very ugly ship.

Nobody will know what happened to the *Andaste* on September 10, 1929, the day a violent gale swept Lake Michigan and caught the boat in the midst of what was to have been a short trip from Grand Haven to Chicago. Some speculated that the old whaleback was done in when its cargo of nineteen hundred tons of gravel shifted, causing the vessel to break up. Others guessed that the crew might have been careless about battening down the ship's hatches for the trip, and the gale generated waves that sank it.

Killed were Capt. Albert L. Anderson and a crew of twenty-four sailors, many of them from Grand Haven. Because there was no radio, the first hint that something happened to the *Andaste* occurred when it failed to arrive at Chicago later in the day. By the next morning, aircraft were searching the lake, and the Coast Guard had boats involved in a search from Chicago, Grand Haven, South Haven, Muskegon and Holland.

Earl Harrington, who lived near Ottawa Beach, told the Coast Guard he watched the lights of a ship a few miles off shore during the storm. He said a powerful sea was up and the ship appeared to be heading toward shore. He said

**The odd-appearing whaleback *Andaste* was lost on Lake Michigan with all hands.**

that while he watched the lights disappeared. Harrington's story was supported on September 13 when the fish tug *Bertha G* discovered wreckage from the *Andaste* about fourteen miles off Ottawa Beach. Among it was a door. George Evans and Joe Collins, crew members who remained behind when the *Andaste* left Grand Haven on her final voyage, identified the door and some attached woodwork. They said it came from Captain Anderson's cabin.

Bodies began floating ashore on the fourth day. Among the pieces of wreckage that eventually drifted in was a plank with a note scribbled in pencil: "Worst storm I have ever been in. Can't stay up much longer. Hope to God we're saved." The note was signed with the initials "A. L. A.," indicating that this was the last message from Captain Anderson.

The bodies recovered the first week were those of Anderson; Capt. Charles Brown, first mate, Grand Haven; Joseph McCadde, second mate, Cleveland; Claude J. Kibby, chief engineer, Fennville, Michigan; Ralph Wiley, second engineer, Benton Harbor; Fred Nienhouse, deckhand, Ferrysburg, Michigan; Thedor Torgeson, wheelsman, Owen, Wisconsin; George Watt, second cook, Grand Haven; M. Green, deckhand, address unknown; William Joslin, fireman, Milwaukee; George Ratcliff, fireman, Grand Haven; L. Godas, fireman, address unknown; Clifford Gould, oiler, Lincoln, Nebraska; Frank Kasperson, watchman, Grand Haven.

# Death Ship *Wisconsin*

In her forty-eight-year history, the thousand-ton propeller *Wisconsin* was a ship fraught with disaster and strange contrasts.

She bore the name *Wisconsin* on the day she was launched in 1881, and still had it on the day she foundered off Kenosha, Wisconsin, in 1929. That was unusual because the boat went through six name changes in between. She bore the name *E. G. Crosby* twice. She was named the *Gen. Robert M. O'Reilly* for one year in between, from 1918 to 1919. Other names were *Naomi* and *Pilgrim*.

The ship burned off Grand Haven on May 21, 1907, with the loss of five lives, and took another sixteen lives when it sank on October 29, 1929. Yet, during World War I, as the *E. G. Crosby*, the same boat was used on the Atlantic coast as a hospital convalescent ship at New York and probably played an important role as a lifesaver.

Even though she went through numerous changes of ownership, a serious fire, was nearly sunk when trapped in ice off Grand Haven in 1885, and was rebuilt several times, the *Wisconsin* ended her career as the same basic ship she was when first launched, a passenger and freight hauler. The *Wisconsin's* first owners, the Goodrich Transit Company of Chicago, were also her last owners. There were four other owners in between.

The two disasters in her history were so terrible that few will remember the many good seasons of faithful service. The *Wisconsin* has gone down in history as a death ship.

The boat was known as the *Naomi* when it burned in 1907, killing four coal passers and one passenger who were caught by the fire while sleeping below deck. It happened at 1:30 AM while the *Naomi,* under the command of Capt. Thomas Traill, was steaming from Grand Haven to Milwaukee with fifty passengers, an estimated thirty crew members and an unknown cargo of freight. The fact that three other ships were nearby averted what could have been an even worse disaster. The steamers *Saxona, Kansas* and *D. G. Kerr,* all converged on the burning ship in time to save lives. It was said a lookout aboard the *Kansas* spotted the fire breaking out aboard the ill-fated boat even before the crew members on the *Naomi* knew.

The Kerr, commanded by a Captain Ballentine, pulled up against the stern of the *Naomi* to take passengers aboard, while the *Saxona,* under command of Capt. George McCollough, picked up survivors from several lifeboats. Rescuers discovered, to their horror, that four crew members were trapped alive below deck in the ship's forecastle with no way of escape. The men, identified only as Gordon, Miner, Stanton and one unknown, were awake and pleading for help through open port holes, where they took turns getting air. The port holes were too small for the men to climb through. "There was no possible means of getting those men out from the red hot steel cage in which they were imprisoned," McCollough said. "Both vessels worked their fire hoses on the burning ship to their full capacity. The cries of the imprisoned men ceased and we heard no more."

The one passenger lost was J. M. Rhoades, a lumber buyer for the Diamond Match Company, Detroit, who was so badly burned that he later died in a Grand Rapids hospital. The *Naomi* was a steel-hulled ship and didn't sink. The burned-out hull was towed by the *Kansas* to Manitowoc, Wisconsin, where the ship was rebuilt.

The second and final disaster happened when the *Wisconsin* developed a serious leak in a northwest gale and sank about seven miles off Kenosha, Wisconsin.

The ship, under command of Capt. H. Dougal Morrison, was steaming from Chicago to Milwaukee with seventy-five passengers and crew members and a cargo of automobiles. First Mate Edward Halverson said he was on deck helping other crew members secure the hatches from the storm when the word came that the ship was taking on a lot of water aft. The cause of the leak was never known. It was determined that the leak was very serious and the ship was in danger of foundering, so Morrison ordered radio operator Kenneth Carlson to signal shore for help. Carlson said he contacted a land station at Chicago, which then telephoned the Coast

**Two disasters marked the forty-eight-year career of the *Wisconsin*. The vessel is remembered as a death ship.**

Guard stations at Racine and Kenosha. He said he kept sending SOS signals until the radio went dead, then got aboard a lifeboat minutes before the *Wisconsin* sank at 7:10 AM.

Coast Guard cutters and the fishing boat *Chambers Brothers* arrived at the scene at about 7:30 AM. They were in time to pluck fifty-nine survivors from the water. Nineteen of those people were later hospitalized. Among the sixteen who died were Morrison and chief engineer Julius Bushman.

# "You'd Better Get Out of Here!"

The steel propeller *Senator* lies on the bottom of Lake Michigan, twenty miles northeast of Port Washington, Wisconsin, with the remains of seven crew members and a cargo of two hundred and forty-one automobiles. The steamer was sunk on the fog shrouded morning of October 31, 1929, when rammed amidships by the steamer *Marquette*.

The *Senator*, commanded by Capt. George Kinch, was on route from Milwaukee to Detroit and the *Marquette*, loaded with iron ore from the steel mills at Indiana Harbor, was bound for Milwaukee. Their courses crossed at 10:40 AM. Nobody was blamed publicly for the accident. It was said the fog was so thick that morning neither ship could see the other until they were within a hundred feet of one another. Capt. W. F. Amesbury, master of the *Marquette*, was criticized for not trying to help the crew of the *Senator* after the boat turned on its port side and sank.

The *Senator* went down in about five minutes; so quickly that crew members barely had time to save themselves. Deckhand William Driscoll of Detroit, who was making his first trip on the lakes, said he was sleeping in his bunk when the *Marquette* drove her bow into the port side of the ship. He said he managed to slip into a shirt and trousers and even strap on a life preserver before he went on deck. By the time he reached the deck, Driscoll said "the ship was listing far over to port. There was no time to get off the boats because the *Senator* was going down right under our feet. We walked right out on her side and into the water. Seven or eight of us swam to a piece of wreckage and hung to it." Seven crew members, including Kinch and assistant steward, Mrs. Matthew Gormley, died.

Wheelsman Herbert Petting said he was with Kinch in the pilot house when the two ships struck. "The captain came in to me after the collision and said: 'Can you swim? You'd better get out of here.'" Petting said he left the wheel and ran to the deck to save himself.

Driscoll said he later saw Kinch walk out with the other men into the water. He said Kinch had a life preserver on, but the ship was starting her dive and he thought the captain got pulled down with it.

Coal passer William Harris said he tried to save Mrs. Gormley. "I met her on the deck. She was hollering. I pulled her up on the side and she and I jumped off. I got on one end of the raft and she caught on the other. The waves turned that raft over twice. They nearly strangled us. Pretty soon Mrs. Gormley called out: 'Help me, help me, help me.' Then she went under."

Radio operator Ralph Ellis said he and two other sailors jumped to the deck of the *Marquette* before it pulled away. The other fifteen survivors were in the water for about an hour after the *Senator* sank. All were picked up by the fishing tug *Delos H. Smith,* which was working nearby and heard the crash.

Petting and second mate Harvey Nicholson charged that the *Marquette* disappeared in the fog and never put out lifeboats. They blamed Amesbury for the loss of many of the other crew members. Amesbury told investigators that he ordered two lifeboats lowered and said he left the bow of his ship lodged in the side of the *Senator* for about ten minutes. He said he thought there was time for the crew to flee aboard the *Marquette* before he pulled away.

Seven sailors died when the *Senator* sank after a collision on Lake Michigan.

The *Marquette's* second mate disputed Amesbury's story. He said Amesbury ordered boats manned, but only because he thought his ship might be sinking. Once it was determined that the *Marquette* was not in any danger, he said the boats were never lowered.

The others who died were first mate John Neilson, second engineer T. A. Ammon, and porter Tony Moreno, all of Detroit; H. J. Grious of Toronto, and Emil Passinger, no address given.

# Ship Out of Control

To coin an old phrase, the Canadian steamer *W. C. Franz* was an accident waiting to happen. Authorities ruled that faulty steering equipment caused the collision that sank the boat off Lake Huron's Thunder Bay on November 21, 1934. An investigation also revealed that defective ropes and tackle at the lifeboats contributed to the deaths of four sailors as they tried to abandon ship.

The *Franz* was rammed and sunk after it unexpectedly turned across the bow of the steamer *Edward E. Loomis* at 3:20 AM. The *Franz* went down by the head while sixteen survivors watched from the deck of the bashed-in *Loomis*.

The *Franz*, under command of seventy-one-year-old Capt. Alec McIntyre of Collingwood, Ontario, unloaded wheat the day before at Port Colborne and was returning empty for another grain cargo at Fort William, Ontario, on Lake Superior. McIntyre was on the bridge most of the day and then turned the ship over to his first mate, James Gobson for the night watch. It was a clear night and the *Franz* was steaming north alongside the steamer *Soreldoc*. Both vessels were belching black coal smoke into the clear night as they steamed along, about thirty miles off the Michigan coast.

Approaching from the north was the *Loomis,* with her first mate, Joseph Lamontague, also standing the night watch. Like McIntyre, Capt. Alex McKenzie, master of the *Loomis,* was asleep in his bunk. Lamontague said he saw the lights of both the *Franz* and *Soreldoc* and sounded signals to let them know the *Loomis* was approaching. Then, just as the three boats all closed in on one another, the *Franz* turned sharply off its course, going directly across the bow of the *Loomis.* "I threw my wheel hard starboard," Lamontague said. "She came right at us and it was impossible to go between the *Franz* and *Soreldoc,* and we hit her."

Officers on the *Franz* said something happened to the steering and the vessel veered out of control at that crucial moment.

**Four died when the *W. C. Franz* was sunk in a collision off Thunder Bay.**

The *Franz's* radio operator A. D. Reeser said he was thrown from his bunk into the bulkhead by the crash. He said he jumped into his clothes, went on deck and sent the first radio message at 3:27 AM. It read: "We are sinking rapidly and taking to the boats." Reeser was also one of the dozen men who were in the starboard lifeboat when a rope failed and ten of the sailors tumbled into the water. "I swam a few strokes until I got to a ladder floating in the water," he said. "I hung on until the *Loomis* lifeboat picked me up."

Three other sailors weren't as lucky. Wheelman Joseph Langridge, who apparently was hurt in the collision, and steward Hugh Woodbeck both disappeared after falling into the water. Chief Engineer A. M. McInnes and cook Norman Matthews grabbed the lifeboat when one end dropped. They were still hanging there, calling for help, when the *Loomis* drew along side. A line was dropped and McInnes was pulled to safety. Matthews lost his grip and fell to his death. The fourth sailor to die was deck hand Francis Granville, who jumped overboard and landed on a floating hatch cover. Companions said Granville had tossed the hatch cover in the water and apparently planned to use it as a raft.

There were conflicting stories about the length of time it took the *Franz* to sink. They ranged from thirty minutes to two hours. The ship apparently was struck in the port bow because it listed first to port and the bow was the first part of the vessel to sink.

It was the second and final collision for the *Franz* in that same part of Lake Huron. The boat was known as the *Uranus* in August, 1906, when it rammed and sank the package freighter *Governor Smith* in fog off Pointe aux Barques.

The *Franz* was built at Wyandotte in 1901. The ship was three hundred forty-six feet long.

# Shipwrecked and Eating Turkey

The men aboard the forty-two-year-old whaleback freighter *Henry W. Cort* knew they were in trouble the night of November 30, 1934, when a gale wracked their ship against the Muskegon breakwall. There they were, trapped in a partly sunken ship, without heat or lights, and no radio with which to report their plight to the outside world.

They made the best of a bad situation. While watching the lights of U. S. Coast Guardsmen risking their lives trying to make a rescue, the twenty-five sailors, under command of Capt. Charles V. Cox, ate leftover Thanksgiving turkey, cranberries and mince pie in the ship's galley. Cox said they were relatively comfortable there, even though the ship was listing to starboard and waves, fanned by sixty-mile-per-hour winds, were sweeping the decks and superstructure. The cabin area was above water and the galley, located on the lee side of the ship, was sheltered.

Things were not going smoothly for Capt. John A. Basch, commander of the Coast Guard crew busy trying to rescue the stranded sailors. Basch sent out a thirty-six-foot powerboat manned by five volunteers at about 10:00 PM, minutes after Coast Guard lookout Orville Peterson reported the ship in distress. The storm capsized the powerboat. Only four of the five guardsmen made it back to shore. Surfman John Dipert drowned.

The survivors of the overturned boat brought important news to Basch, however. They said they got close enough to confirm that the cabin area in the *Cort's* stern was still above water and there was hope that the sailors on the ship were alive and even sheltered. When dawn came, Basch brought guardsmen from Muskegon and the nearby Grand Haven stations to the breakwall, where a second daring rescue effort was started.

Lashing themselves together like mountain climbers, the guardsmen worked their way over the slippery boulders that made up the breakwater, while fierce waves rolled over

The whaleback *Henry W. Cort* lies wrecked against the Muskegon breakwater in 1934.

them. When they got close to the *Cort,* they shot a line to the ship and then set up a breeches buoy to remove the stranded sailors. The men were then brought off the wreck, one-at-a-time, to the breakwater.

With everybody strapped together, the sailors and guardsmen carefully worked their way back off the rocks to safety. Everybody walked away except Harry Sutton, Detroit, the ship's sixty-year-old cook, who collapsed on the breakwater. They said first mate Harvey Mathews of Croswell, Michigan, picked Sutton up and carried him the rest of the way.

The *Cort* was engaged in carrying cargo between Chicago, Michigan City, Holland and Muskegon. It left Holland at 9:00 AM Friday, empty, bound for South Chicago. "There was a stiff southerly wind when we started," said Captain Cox. "We were a few miles off Michigan City when the gale struck. We could make no headway in it, so I decided we'd have to do one of two things: either try to beach her or try to make the harbor at Muskegon. We ran for Muskegon, about a hundred miles north."

For a while it looked as if the *Cort* was going to slip right into the harbor. "I was congratulating myself upon having made it, when a huge wave struck her and piled her up on the tip of the north arm of the breakwater. She began to fill with water in five minutes. I ordered all hands on deck and made them put on life preservers," Cox said.

He said the boat immediately listed forty-five degrees to starboard and he thought for a while that it might roll to its side and then sink in deep water. "Then I began to fear that the boilers might explode. When the lights went out, we knew that the water had doused the fires. And, when it appeared that the superstructure was going to remain above water, I invited the crew into the galley where we remained all night."

The *Cort* was never salvaged. Storms continued to batter the stricken ship until she broke in two. It was scrapped the next year. The *Cort* originally was the *Pillsbury* when launched at Superior, Wisconsin, in 1892.

# The Tug That Disappeared

One of the many lost wrecks lying on the cluttered bottom of Lake Huron near Pointe aux Barques is the mystery tugboat *Fred A. Lee*. This boat foundered November 13, 1936 about thirteen miles northeast of the light during broad daylight and in sight of an officer on a passing freighter.

Nobody knows why the *Lee* sank, or why the entire crew of five sailors disappeared so quickly with her. A sea was running that afternoon, but it wasn't considered serious enough to have caused a stout old boat like the *Fred A. Lee* to break up and plunge to the bottom so quickly that it trapped its crew. There was speculation that the boiler exploded.

Capt. Theodore Dahlburg said he had his ship, the stone carrier *Munson,* on the scene within fifteen minutes after his first mate, Donald Mauts, watched the tug disappear at 4:28 PM. Dahlburg said all that was found was splintered wreckage from a ship's cabin, a chair, mattress, pillows and a life preserver.

Lost with the *Lee* were Capt. Achille Renaud, of Amherstburg, Ontario; chief engineer Cecil Smale of Port Stanley, Ontario; second engineer Archie Gibb of Corunna, Ontario; fireman P. Titus and wheelsman Roy McDonald, both of Sarnia. The men were taking the tug on its last trip of the season from Wallaceburg, Ontario, where it had been chartered for the summer by a sand and gravel company, to winter quarters at Sault Ste. Marie. The *Lee* was owned by Capt. T. B. Climie of Sault Ste. Marie.

McDonald was not a regular member of the *Lee's* crew. He shipped out for the ride, probably because his boat was already laid up for the season and he saw it as a way to pick up some extra cash. It was a fatal decision.

There were clues supporting the explosion theory. Dahlburg said the splintered wreckage and the speed at which the tug disappeared from sight led him to believe the vessel blew up. Also, it was learned that the Harbor Beach Coast Guard pulled the *Lee* off a reef or sand bar near Harbor Beach

**Some believe the Canadian tug *Fred A. Lee* blew up on Lake Huron.**

at about 11:00 AM that same day. They said the *Lee* went aground the night before and spent several hours on the bar before help came.

The Coast Guard speculated that the grounding may have damaged the tug's wooden hull, causing a leak. They said cold water may have gotten to the boiler causing it to explode. Owner Climie carried that theory even farther. He said the tug may have been churning mud up from the lake bottom while trying to work it's way free from the reef. If that mud was sucked into the boilers, it could have caused valves to stick and set off a chain reaction and cause the explosion. The truth may never be known.

# Capsized on Georgian Bay

Seven people died when the motorship *Hibou* capsized and sank off Owen Sound, Ontario, on November 21, 1936. Seas were rolling that morning but nobody expected trouble. The *Hibou* was a seasoned craft of twenty-nine years and had made this trip many times before. Some of the off duty crew members were sleeping in their cabin below deck.

It was the last trip of the season and the boat was loaded with general provisions, including flour, canned goods, hay, oil and even a sewing machine to help the residents of Manitoulin Island get through the coming winter.

Deckhand Scotty Smart suggested that a stalled engine might have caused the ship to capsize. (Authorities later blamed an improperly stored cargo.) Smart said the ship was rolling but taking the seas all right at first. "Suddenly as we rounded the point the engines stopped. The boat lurched and then turned over. Most of us were in our pajamas below decks, and I think those who are missing were trapped below."

He said ten of the seventeen people aboard escaped by clinging to a life raft. Everybody hung on the raft in the unbearably cold water until they paddled a half mile to shore. It seemed like a long time because the survivors were suffering from the weather. There were no oars so they paddled with their hands. "We shouted to each other to keep up our courage and tried to keep warm by kicking our legs and slapping each other's arms," Smart said. Had they been much longer in the water, there might have been more casualties. Many of the survivors were removed unconscious from the water and some had frozen arms and legs.

Capt. Norman McKay was among the dead. Smart said he was last seen standing on one side of the overturned boat, firing flares. He disappeared when the *Hibou* sank about five miles from Owen Sound. Also listed as dead were Iona Johnston, stewardess; Raymond Earls, cook; and deckhands Guy McReynolds, Murdock McIvor, Edward Dunham and Jack Mimard.

The *Hibou* was owned by the Dominion Transportation Company Limited of Owen Sound. She was serving as a freight and passenger ferry that season between Owen Sound and Manitoulin Island.

The wreck was raised by United Towing and Salvage Company in 1942 and towed to Montreal for rebuilding. Divers said the boat was ninety feet down and badly damaged. They said the smoke stack was collapsed to the deck. The steel wheel house, captain's room and cabins in the bow were still intact, but the wooden cabins and dining hall on the first deck had collapsed.

The vessel later was sold to Tocutex Societa Anonime of Honduras and sailed on the ocean until it foundered in 1953 during a trip from Panama to Buenos Aries.

The *Hibou* capsized on Georgian Bay in 1936. Seven people were killed.

# "All American Hero"

The seventeen survivors of the shipwreck *Novadoc* would tell you without reservation that Pentwater fisherman Clyde Cross was an all-American hero. But when Cross and helpers Gustave Fisher and Joe Fountain were driving their ancient fish tug *The Three Brothers* into mountain-high seas to reach the stranded freighter, their critics were calling them fearless daredevils.

That's because Cross was going where Coast Guardsmen feared to go. He put the lives of himself and his crew in jeopardy to try to save men who had been trapped and battered aboard the *Novadoc* at Juniper Beach for nearly thirty-six hours and were in danger of waiting at least another day before help could reach them.

As it were, two men had already been washed overboard and the ship's mate, Capt. R. A. Simpell, noted in the logbook that others would be dead if they weren't rescued before nightfall. "We kept shooting rockets up until finally about ten o'clock we saw a boat coming down the coast . . . it was a grand sight," Simpell said.

The *Novadoc* was one of three big lake carriers lost in the same area of Lake Michigan during the Armistice Day Storm of November 11, 1940. The others, the *William B. Davock* and *Anna C. Minch* disappeared with all hands. Two fishing tugs foundered off South Haven and several other vessels were driven ashore in the blow which claimed an estimated one hundred and fifty-nine lives.

The *Novadoc* was a Canadian ship under command of Capt. Donald Steip. She was on her way from Chicago to Montreal with a load of carbon coke when the northwesterly gale drove the ship into the Michigan shore.

"We ordered all our boys to put on lifebelts and come to the bridge as we could see that nothing could save the ship," Simpell said. "The captain thought if he put the engines in reverse, perhaps we could keep clear . . . but we were getting closer to the beach. Then all at once the ship was in the back-

The *Novadoc* was one of the casualties of the Armistice Day Storm of 1940. The crew escaped.

wash from the shore and of her own accord, she turned around, heading out into the lake. The captain put the engines full speed ahead. Then things happened so quickly one could scarcely follow them." Simpell said the ship was struck by a series of powerful seas that broke out the five pilot house windows and knocked everybody to the deck. "The captain stopped the engines," he said. "Just then the ship struck the shoals with a shock that shook her from one end to the other, keeping it up until she was finally banging up against the bank about five hundred feet from shore and about one and one-quarter miles from Little Sable Light."

Crew members were forced off the bridge into the captain's quarters to get out of the water. There, everybody laughed and joked about their situation and waited for help to arrive.

Seven others sailors, the engine room crew and the cooks, didn't fare as well. They were all caught in the after-end of the ship where the seas continued to flood their quarters. Everybody stood knee-deep in ice cold water, bailing for their lives with pails. The men tossed water out of the broken port holes while the waves dumped it back in again. They had enough by Wednesday morning on the second day. That was when everybody from the after part of the ship tried to crawl across the ice-coated and storm-tossed decks to reach the ship's bow. All but the cooks, identified as Joseph Deshaw of Toronto and Phillip Falvin, Halifax, Nova Scotia, made it. Deshaw and Falvin disappeared during the perilous trip. If they could have waited a few more hours, rescue was on the way.

That was when Clyde Cross saved the day. After Cross brought the survivors smartly into port, something happened that may have been remembered even more than the rescue. It made the story a legend in lake lore. After stepping safely ashore Captain Steip gratefully reached in his breast pocked and produced a roll of bills, which he offered to Cross.

Nobody will ever know how much money the roll contained. That's because Cross leaned back against the bulkhead of his tired old tug, while the automobile engine that drove her still clanked noisily beneath his feat, and said: "Hell no, captain. Glad to be of service."

# Runaway Barge

The eighteen sailors on the two hundred fifty-foot tanker tow barge *Cleveco* were in a terrible fix. It was early on the morning of December 2, 1942, somewhere on raging Lake Erie.

The *Cleveco*, laden with twenty-four thousand barrels of fuel oil, was wallowing violently in a serious winter storm, she was taking on water, and her six hundred-foot long tow line was leading off into the gale to the stern of the tug *Admiral*, which was lying on the bottom of the lake.

Capt. William H. Smith, Cleveland, had radioed for help within minutes after the accident. The Coast Guard was sending a rescue vessel, but Smith knew there wasn't much anybody could do until the gale was over. The waves were pounding the ice coated decks. By the way the vessel was tossing, he knew that no man could live for long in such a sea, and no one dared to attempt a transport from the barge to another ship.

Smith hoped, for the sake of his ship and his crew, that the storm was going to ease very soon. "Water is coming in through the hawse pipe and flooding the forecastle around the anchor windlass and is gaining in height. If it rises over the fourteen-inch sill to the deck level it is feared it will flood the donkey boilers and generators, putting the communication and heating systems out of order," he radioed to the Cleveland Coast Guard. That turned out to be the last message received from the barge.

The *Cleveco* was being towed by the tug *Admiral* from Toledo to Cleveland when the gale caught them. Nobody knows for sure what happened aboard the *Admiral*, but one radio message from Smith indicated the tug got its propeller fouled with the tow line and capsized at about 4:00 AM. The tug sank unexpectedly, taking Capt. John O. Swanson, of River Rouge, Michigan, and thirteen other sailors to their death. Everything happened so fast that the tug never sent a radio message. It was up to Smith to send the bad news. He said

The tanker barge *Cleveco* sank with all hands in a storm on Lake Erie.

his location was about fifteen miles northwest of Cleveland. As soon as word reached the Cleveland Coast Guard station, Chief Boatswain's Mate John Needham and three other guardsmen, Arthur R. Nash, John C. Lavinsky, and James E. Belisle, set out in a motor lifeboat. Needham had a very personal interest in this disaster. He was a cousin to nineteen-year-old John Tierney, Cleveland, a wheelman on the *Admiral*. His boat battled the seas all that morning, searching the waters for any sign of survivors from the missing tug, or the drifting barge.

By the time Needham's boat arrived at the scene, the *Cleveco* had either broken her tow line or the crew cut it loose in an effort to improve their chances in the storm. Anchors were not holding and the barge was drifting east before the wind. Captain Smith's radio messages were still being received, but where was the barge? The Coast Guard Cutters *Ossipee* and *Crocus,* and a second motor lifeboat from the Lorain, Ohio station also joined in the search. Two Civil Air Patrol pilots, Clare Livingston and Marilyn Miller, took small planes out into the storm that morning in an attempt to find the runaway barge. Livingston got lucky. She radioed the ship's position about twelve miles east of where the *Admiral* went down. It wasn't long before the *Ossipee* was standing by. But the storm refused to let up and rescue was impossible. At 3:30 PM the *Cleveco's* radio went silent just as the two ships were caught in a blinding snowstorm. The temperature at the Cleveland Coast Guard stationed registered fourteen degrees and it was still falling.

Nobody knows what horrors the crew of the *Cleveco* experienced that day and the night that followed. The sinking barge was out of power, which meant that there was no heat. Even though she had no engines, the *Cleveco* was designed much like a bulk freighter, with pilot house in the bow and galley and living quarters at the stern. That meant that some of the men were separated by the long ice-coated deck in between, which probably made their plight even worse.

The Coast Guard stood helplessly by at sundown as the storm continued to rage. It was obvious that only a miracle would keep the barge afloat until dawn. There was no miracle. The *Cleveco* disappeared sometime around 1:00 AM. The vessel broke up and sank, taking Smith and his entire crew down with it. Six bodies were found in the water around a large oil slick. A total of thirty-two sailors perished in the twin sinkings, making it one of the worst disasters of modern times.

# Killer Fire at Toronto

Sanford Newman was making the most out of the late season excursion aboard the Canada Steamship Liner *Noronic*. Newman and his wife were among the five hundred twenty-four passengers taking advantage of a special off-season rate to make the autumn cruise in 1949. The vessel arrived at the Toronto dock on Friday evening, September 16, and was scheduled to leave at 7:00 AM the following day on the last leg of the trip through the Thousand Islands. The *Noronic* never made that trip. It burned at the dock that night, killing an estimated hundred thirty-nine people.

The trip was to have been the last hurrah of summer for many of the passengers, who partied well into the night. Others went ashore to take in some of Toronto's colorful night life. Survivors said those aboard the ship were making it a gala occasion, and keeping the ship's bars busy. There was heavy drinking.

The Newmans, who were traveling with a group of friends from Cleveland, were enjoying a more sober kind of party in a parlor on C-Deck, somewhere amidships. They were broken up into small groups for a hot game of cards. With the Newman's were Mr. and Mrs. Harry Waxman, Mr. and Mrs. Ernest Bernstein, Mr. and Mrs. Edward Sherman, and Mr. and Mrs. Jack Feingold, all of Cleveland. Their enthusiasm for cards probably saved their lives.

Newman thought it was about 2:30 AM when he heard a commotion in the hall and someone smelled smoke. "I was among the men who went to the rear of the boat to find out what it was." As he walked along the starboard corridor Newman said the smell of smoke got very strong. "We found the fire in what may have been a linen closet on the (port) side of the ship. Two bus boys were already there trying to put it out with a fire extinguisher. I heard one of them say, 'You'd better go and get help' to the other one. Then the smoke choked me up. I ran back to the parlor to warn the others."

The *Noronic* fire at Toronto was among the worst of the modern Great Lakes disasters. One hundred thirty-nine people perished.

Because they were awake and warned in time, the Cleveland card players all escaped the disaster that was to follow.

Another witness to the scene outside the burning linen closet was Ben Kosman, a Cleveland businessman, who also was traveling with friends. "I was just going along the passageway when I smelled smoke. Then I saw a couple of the bell boys coming along with fire extinguishers. So I went along to the cabin about in the center. They opened the door. They shouldn't have done that. The flames roared out. They might have been trying to put out hell with their fountain pens. It was no use, and they couldn't, or didn't close the door again." Kosman said.

The fire swept the ship so quickly that many passengers were trapped in their cabins. Some were believed to have died in their sleep, never realizing that the ship was on fire. Bedlam broke out. Survivors told of magnificent acts of heroism as well as dark stories of cowardice as people rushed to escape the smoke-filled corridors. Capt. William Taylor was counted among the heroes. Survivors told a board of inquiry how Taylor was seen among the crew members, fighting the fire with water. Then, when he realized that the fire was out of control, Taylor ran along the deck smashing windows and portholes, helping trapped passengers get out of their cabins when fire blocked normal exits through the doors to the inside passageways.

Steward Chic Yates said he was with Taylor during a search of the ship's cabins. "We checked the steward's quarters, the engine room and the cabins. Everybody was out. On the way back it was really bad. Sparks were flying and the smoke was thick. I tripped over a woman who was lying across the passageway. The captain and I carried her to the side of the ship. We tied a rope around her and lowered her into a launch. People were jumping over the side. Then we took one last look. We couldn't do any more. The ship was ablaze to the superstructure," Yates said. Taylor was treated for exhaustion and burns aboard the *Kingston,* a sister ship docked nearby. His burns apparently were serious because the official inquiry was delayed for several days until he was well enough to testify.

Sylvia Carpenter, Detroit, said she was trying to help people climb off the burning ship to the dock below. "Someone had thrown a rope ladder over the dockside, but it was all tangled up. Then a rope was tossed over the rail. I put a hitch knot in it to hold it to a stanchion. As I did, three men pushed in front of me and shoved some screaming women out of the way. The men went down the rope. After that, Carpenter said she helped the other women climb to safety before escaping herself.

Elsewhere on the ship, people were exhibiting blind hysteria. Alberta Agala, Detroit, said "the *Noronic's* A-Deck was a complete scene of panic. There was a mob of men and women surging back and forth. Men were pushing women around and many were knocked to the floor. There was so much panic I don't know how these people got segregated to find a way to safety. I slid down a rope." C. E. Metcal of Columbus, O., said he watched people jump from the ship, some to their death. "It was terrible. Some of the people who jumped landed on the dock far below. Others landed in the water. The police and firemen did a marvelous job using boats to rescue the people who leaped into the water," he said.

There were horror stories from people who were nearly trapped to die in their cabins. Mrs. Mat J. Hackman of Covington, Kentucky, said she "woke up about 2:00 AM and the room was all ablaze, and smoke was everywhere. I screamed to my husband to wake up. The heat was terrible, and the people were screaming all about us. We got outside on the deck and jumped overboard into the water. I could see people still jumping into the water, and some of them were on fire."

Emil Dahlke, Hazel Park, Michigan, said he and his wife were awakened in their cabin by someone pounding on the door. "I heard the awful word, 'Fire!' ringing down the alleyways. It sent a chill through me. I flung open our cabin door and was met by a blast of heat and flame. I ran back into our cabin for my wife and for a few moments we just stood there. I could see the horror on her face. There was no time to dress. We ran to the stateroom window and pushed out the screen. A deckhand grabbed our shoulders and pulled us through the small port hole. Hundreds were rushing around the ship screaming and crying out for their relatives and friends. It was complete panic and women were knocked down in the struggle. All I could think of was getting my wife from the inferno. We ran to the side of the ship and I slid down a hawser with my wife on my shoulder."

When the fire was out, the ship was no more than a partly sunken hulk of smoldering ruin. *Toronto Star* reporter Edwin Feeney was the first newsman allowed aboard on the following day. He wrote: "It was a horrible picture of charred remains amid foot-deep embers and melted glass. There wasn't a wooden partition standing. There was no wooden furniture or upholstery unburned. No stairways remained save one at the bow of the ship. Every pane of glass had been melted by the intense heat. Fire Chief Art Smith said his men found victims in every position. Many had their lives snuffed out without waking. One young woman, wrapped in a blanket, had her face burned, but her body was not touched. Upper bunks fell crashing down on victims below. Firemen searching the ruins found human remains between scorched mattresses. Priests from St. Michael's Cathedral, Father Vincent Foy and Father Bernard Kyte, stepped about the debris, sometimes almost knee deep. The steel stanchions were bent in every shape. The decks crumpled and buckled from the heat, made progress hazardous for the firemen seeking the dead."

The death toll was estimated at a hundred thirty-nine, although nobody knew for sure. The figure varies among the records of the day.

As the world agonized over the tragedy, investigations were started into the cause of the fire and loss of so many lives. It was determined that the fire either started in the linen closet on C-Deck, or in an adjoining women's restroom, possibly from a carelessly tossed cigarette.

Officials discovered that the crew members who first discovered the fire lost precious minutes trying to fight the fire on their own before sounding an alarm. The alarm was only sent to the bridge and other key parts of the ship. Nobody sounded a general alarm that would have aroused the passengers. Investigators also learned that no alarm was given the Toronto Fire Department by the crew, and the ship's water lines had not been connected with city water mains at the dock. Of a crew of a hundred and seventy, only sixteen were on duty when the fire broke out. All of the crew members who were familiar with the ship and knew the escape routes got off alive.

In spite of his acts of heroism, Captain Taylor shouldered blame for the failures. He lost his license for one year for failing to provide proper leadership. The Canadian government also was criticized for allowing the ship to operate without fireproof bulkheads and an automatic fire alarm system. Damage suits were settled about three years later for over two million dollars.

# The Liner That Got Off Course

Capt. Rudolph J. Kiessling admitted to a board of inquiry that he usually ran the passenger liner *City of Cleveland III* a few miles out of the normal traffic lanes. He explained that the *Cleveland* was a fast ship and he was afraid she would overrun slower moving freighters heading in the same direction.

Some folks thought Kiessling took his command a little too far off the normal track on Sunday, June 25, 1950, when he put it on a collision course with the Norwegian freighter *Ravnefjneel* on Lake Huron, just off Harbor Beach. Four people died when the *Ravnefjneel* slid out of the fog and rammed the *Cleveland's* port side, near the stern, at 6:16 AM.

All of the dead and injured were on the *Cleveland,* which was carrying eighty-nine passengers on an annual Benton Harbor, Michigan Chamber of Commerce cruise. The excursion was bound for Detroit where members planned to attend the Detroit-New York baseball game that same afternoon.

The damaged liner *City of Cleveland III* following a 1950 collision near Harbor Beach.

Killed were Benton Harbor police chief Alvin Boyd; Merwyn Stouck, former mayor of Benton Harbor and president of the Lockway-Stouck Paper Company; Louis Patitucci, owner of a South Bend, Indiana, frozen food company, and Frank Skelly, a Benton Harbor automobile dealer. Several other passengers were injured as the men were jostled from the shock of the collision. Some were hurled bodily through windows and at least one of the dead men, Merwyn Stouck, flew off the deck and into the water. Friends said Stouck was in the habit of taking an early morning walk and was on the deck when the freighter hit the *Cleveland*. The force of the crash threw him over the rail. He was pulled from the water alive, but died a few hours later in Harbor Beach Community Hospital.

Another passenger, Dr. C. J. Oceran, said the cruise seemed to have been jinxed from the start. Oceran said the ship was in fog from the time it left port on Thursday and had been wandering around for two days in the middle of Lake Michigan waiting for the fog to lift.

Captain Kiessling came under severe criticism for the way in which he was operating the ship. Chief Boatswain's Mate Kenneth Call, commander of the Harbor Beach Coast Guard station, said he was told by the crew of the *Ravnefjneel* that the freighter's radar tracked the *Cleveland* at four miles off shore. Call said the rules of the road required southbound vessels to travel ten miles off shore at that point. He said the northbound lane, in which the *Ravnefjneel* was traveling, was four miles off shore.

Ironically, the owners of the *Cleveland III* removed her radar equipment that season. The type of radar she carried had been pronounced substandard by the Federal Communications Commission and it was not replaced.

It also was learned in hearings that Kiessling was running his command at almost top speed at sixteen miles an hour in the fog. Officials noted that he violated Pilot Rule Thirteen, which requires vessels to slow to bare steerage way when the fog signal is received.

Kiessling said he heard the signals from the freighter, but thought the vessel was headed south in the same direction as the *Cleveland*. He said that from his own calculations, he believed he was in the southbound lane and was at least ten miles off shore.

The *Ravnefjneel* was only slightly damaged. It continued on its way to Milwaukee.

Even though the *Cleveland* proceeded to Detroit under its own power after the accident, the boat never sailed again. The vessel remained tied up at Detroit and then Windsor for three years. Vandals caused extensive damage. Then during a storm in June, 1953, the *Cleveland* was wrenched loose from the moorings and it floated off in the Detroit River until grounding at Hennepin Point.

The ship was sold to Carl Ventimiglia, who planned to convert the hull for use as a crane barge. While workers were preparing to dismantle the vessel at Windsor, it caught fire and burned to a total wreck on October 20, 1954.

# Bad Omens for the *Steinbrenner*

When the freighter *Henry Steinbrenner* foundered in a Lake Superior gale in the spring of 1953, she took seventeen sailors and a slice of Michigan history to the bottom with her.

The *Steinbrenner* was among a long list of fine boats built in the old Jenks Shipyard at Port Huron. Her nearly finished hull was on the ways when the yard was destroyed by fire on March 19, 1901. Firemen trained their hoses on the ship to save it. It is said that sailors are a most superstitious people. If that is true, there is little doubt that they saw the fire as a very bad omen. Indeed the boat left behind a dark record. Not only were her builders nearly put out of business by the fire, the *Steinbrenner* was sunk after a collision on Mud Lake in 1909, the ship was involved in a second crash on Superior's Whitefish Bay in 1923, and in the end it took seventeen unlucky sailors to their deaths when it foundered on Lake Superior in 1953.

The first collision was with the steamer *Berwind,* another hard-luck vessel that ran a string of two more collisions after her name was changed to the *Parker Evans.* The *Berwind* hit the starboard bow of the *Steinbrenner* during a blinding snow storm on the night of December 5. The *Steinbrenner* was downbound with seven thousand tons of iron ore in her hold. The crash tore open the hull and the ship settled to the bottom of the lake.

Most of the crew got away in the ship's boat, which was located on the stern. Captain Lohr, the second mate, and Freeman Isaacs, the ship's wheelman, were caught in the wheel house so they went down with the ship. Fortunately, Mud Lake is very shallow so the *Steinbrenner* didn't go down very far. When it came to rest, the wheelhouse and much of the forward cabins were still above the water.

As the ship sank, the lights went out, and Captain Lohr realized he and his ship were in a very dangerous situation. "For a long time we were without a light, and several vessels downbound were headed straight toward us. At times

Seventeen sailors died when the *Henry Steinbrenner* foundered on Lake Superior.

I thought they would run us down. I shouted until I got hoarse. They heard and moved out a little. One big fellow came within twenty feet of us," he recalled. Crew members found a kerosene lamp and got it lit as a warning to approaching ships. It was only then that Lohr agreed to leave his command and board a waiting boat from the nearby anchored *Berwind.*

The crew members who escaped in the lifeboat pulled against the storm to nearby Round Island, where they built a fire and tried to get under as much shelter from the snow as possible. The fire was noticed by the keeper of Round Island light, who brought the men to his home for the night.

The *Berwind* was severely damaged and leaking badly, but it did not sink. The ship lay alongside the *Steinbrenner* until the next morning, then steamed south to Detour.

The *Steinbrenner's* second collision was small potatoes compared to her other misfortunes. She bumped with the propeller *John McCartney Kennedy* in Whitefish Bay while making her way through heavy fog on October 11, 1923. Neither vessel was sunk. The damage to the *Steinbrenner* was estimated at five thousand dollars.

The Steinbrenner spent its last forty-four years as a faithful workhorse. For a while it seemed as if her bad luck days were over. As all superstitious sailors will tell you, a boat like the *Steinbrenner* was not about to end its days in a wrecking yard. Her violent end during a raging Lake Superior gale was probably the way it was meant to be.

Some of the surviving crew members told a board of inquiry in Cleveland that they felt the *Steinbrenner* was old and unseaworthy, and never should have been out on the lake. The fifty-two-year-old boat was loaded to the Plimsoll lines with iron ore when it steamed out of Duluth harbor early on Sunday, May 10. As the vessel approached the center of the lake, a great storm front which brought snow, tornadoes and heavy rains across the Midwest began lashing Lake Superior. The *Steinbrenner* struggled in the storm against building waves. Capt. Albert Stiglin said he thought the seas got to a height of twenty feet and winds blew as high as seventy miles an hour. By 7:00 AM Monday, Stiglin sent distress calls and reported the boat's big hatch covers failing.

Stiglin later said the boat was wallowing in the huge waves, the decks were awash, and the winds were actually tearing some of the ship's huge wooden hatch covers away. Four or five hatch covers went, all of them in the after part of the boat. Once they were gone, nothing stopped the seas from flooding the hold.

The captain's story was rebutted by watchman Norman M. Bragg, who told the board of inquiry that the threads were stripped on the number eleven hatch and this caused it to tear open while the vessel was off Isle Royal at about 7 AM Sunday. "We were taking water something awful for nearly twelve hours before she went down," Bragg said.

Only fourteen of the boat's crew of thirty-one survived. Stiglin said everybody was still on board when the *Steinbrenner* sank. "We just rode the lifeboats off the deck."

He said the men died of exposure in the boats before they were picked up by the freighters *Frederick Sykes,* the *Joseph F. Thompson* and the *D. M. Clemson.* Some of the men suffered from broken arms and legs. Survivors praised third engineer Arthur Morse, who jumped at the last second from a lifeboat to cut a line to the sinking freighter so the boat could get away. Morse never made it back to the boat. He went down with the ship.

## Blaze of Glory

The old steamer *Put-In-Bay* went out in a blaze of glory on Lake St. Clair on October 4, 1953. It was planned that way. The wooden decks were drenched with fuel and then the ship's last master, Capt. Fred Becker, tossed a burning torch.

An estimated twenty thousand spectators stood in the night rain on nearby Metropolitan Beach to witness the passage of this once proud excursion vessel. Hundreds more packed a fleet of personal pleasure boats that anchored around the burning ship. As the flames swept the wooden superstructure, the boats sounded their whistles and horns as a final tribune.

Some thought it was a fitting end for a ship that gave pleasure to so many people in her day. Other's weren't so sure. Reporter Mark Weichsler, in a story for the *Times Herald* at nearby Port Huron, said he sensed a sadness among the crowd. "There was no laughter . . . Even the skies were weeping," Weichsler said about the rain.

Before it was burned, the ship was stripped of nautical trappings. Everything was sold to souvenir hunters at a

**The proud steamer *Put-In-Bay* goes up in flames on Lake St. Clair.**

The *Put-In-Bay* steams proudly down the Detroit River during better times.

store near the Detroit waterfront. The ship resembled a tattered ruin in her last hours. Old papers, debris from by-gone days, pieces of the ship leftover after the stripping work was finished, were scattered around on the decks. Windows were left broken. Doors swinging ajar. A flag was flying at full mast when the fires were kindled.

The two hundred sixty-six-foot pleasure ship hauled thousands of passengers between Port Huron, Detroit and Sandusky, Ohio from the time she was built in 1911. But the *Put-In-Bay* was a casualty of age and changing times. When business dropped, the ship was idled at Detroit in 1951. Two years later, it was sold at public auction for eleven thousand dollars.

The new owner, David C. Lowe, president of Detroit Marine Terminals, decided to scrap the ship. He got permission from the U. S. Coast Guard to burn the wooden superstructure before having the steel hull cut up. Lowe didn't attend the burning. "I can't bear to see it," he said.

# "The Ship is Breaking Up!"

The U. S. Steel Corporation freighter *Carl D. Bradley* held two records in her time. At six hundred twenty-three feet in length, she was the largest ship afloat on the Great Lakes when launched in 1927. And the *Bradley* was the largest ship to ever sink on the lakes when it went down during a Lake Michigan gale on November 18, 1958.

The *Bradley's* loss, and the thirty-three men who died with her, are counted among the modern tragedies on the lakes. Nearly all of the victims lived in the small Michigan lakefront town of Rogers City. There were two survivors.

The ship broke up and sank without warning that afternoon while pounding her way northward against the gale from Gary, Indiana, toward Rogers City. The *Bradley,* under the command of Capt. Roland Bryan, had delivered limestone at Gary and was returning empty when it ran into a storm packing sixty-mile-per-hour winds.

The ship foundered so quickly that the crew barely had time to signal a "mayday" radio message before it was all over. It was at 5:31 PM that Charles Petitt, radio operator at the Charlevoix, Michigan, Coast Guard station heard the signal: "Mayday, mayday, mayday. This is the *Carl D. Bradley.* Our position is approximately twelve miles southwest of Gull Island. We are in serious trouble." Petitt said there was a moment's silence. "Then, I could hear someone shouting, 'Run, grab life jackets. Get the jackets.' Then, there was another 'mayday' and 'the ship is breaking up.'"

The man sending those signals was first mate Elmer Fleming who later said he didn't know if the hastily made radio call had been heard by anybody. He had no way of realizing it at the moment, but his radio call probably saved his own life, plus the life of deckhand Frank Mayes. The message launched a major sea and air search that led to a Coast Guard recovery the next morning of the open life raft that Fleming and Mayes were sharing. They were the only survivors.

Fleming said he was working in the pilot house with Captain Bryan when the trouble started. "I heard a heavy

194

**Two crew members on the *Carl D Bradley* lived to tell how the ship foundered during a Lake Michigan gale.**

thud from somewhere in the ship and an alarm bell began to clang. I spun around and looked back aft down the deck. I saw the stern of the boat was sagging and knew we were in trouble." After sending distress signals, Fleming said he stepped out on deck and was starting to inspect a raft located near the pilot house when the ship turned over on its side and threw both him and the raft in the water together.

Mayes said he was working below deck when the ship started breaking up. He said he ran up on deck at the first alarm, just in time to also be flung into the water as the *Bradley* went over. He came to the surface a few feet from Fleming's raft and managed to get aboard.

"We looked back and the ship and saw the stern go straight down," Fleming said. "There was an explosion when the last part of the stern went under. That was when the water hit the boilers."

Two other sailors joined Fleming and Mayes on the raft, but both were lost during the night when the raft was tipped upside down several times by the angry seas. "After the first flip, Fleming and I were the only persons to make it back and we were alone the rest of the time," Mayes said. "I was never so cold in my life." The raft was a redwood platform twelve feet by five and one-half feet, built on two parallel steel tanks. There was a three-inch high railing on which was attached rope handlines. Mayes said he did a lot of praying that night, while holding on to the handlines and waiting for dawn. It was so cold, he said his hands got numb and ice was forming on his hair and jacket. His prayers were answered. When the Coast Guard rescue ship *Sundew* picked them up after fourteen hours in the water, both men were suffering from exposure, but were in remarkably good condition after their ordeal.

The *Bradley* lies in three hundred sixty feet of water about five and three-quarter miles northwest of Boulder Reef.

# Tanker Blast at Sarnia

The people of Sarnia, Ontario, on the St. Clair River, still remember the morning of September 4, 1961, when the gasoline tanker *Imperial Hamilton* blew up.

The explosion happened just before 8:00 AM. It rocked the Imperial Oil Company dock, shattering windows and knocking down nearby warehouses. Workers on the ship were hurled several feet through the air, but miraculously, no one was killed. Three sailors were hospitalized and two others treated at a Sarnia hospital before they were released.

The explosion was centered in the after hold of the two hundred fifty-foot-long tanker. It tore a large hole in the side of the vessel, ripped away a hundred and fifty feet of the dock and destroyed a small storage building. A spectacular fire, fed by four thousand barrels of gasoline in number four and number five holds, ravaged the ship for hours before it was brought under control.

The *Imperial Hamilton* arrived Sunday, the day before the blast, from Sault Ste. Marie, Ontario, and was load-

The gasoline tanker *Imperial Hamilton* exploded and burned at Sarnia on the St. clair River.

ing gasoline for delivery at Cutler, Ontario, when the explosion occurred. Nobody could decide what caused it. Some speculated that vapor from the gasoline got into the engine room and ignited when the ship's boilers were fired. Company officials said the day was hot and humid, and the fumes from the gasoline being pumped into the tanker apparently were settling in the empty hold and not getting away. The vapors were turning the *Imperial Hamilton* into a bomb waiting to go off. All it took was a spark.

Hospitalized were Eugene Pyne, fourth engineer, and Edward Quinn, fireman, both from Sarnia; and Roland Frenette, second engineer, Montreal. Treated for injuries were Joseph Croston, chief cook, from Collingwood, Ontario, and Gilbert Johnson, assistant cook, Toronto, Ontario. Johnson said he was just putting a pumpkin pie in the oven when the blast threw him over the sink.

The *Hamilton* did not sink. The burned out hull remained at Sarnia until it was stripped the following year. The pilot house was removed to Courtright, Ontario, where it became a marine museum. The hull was sunk as a temporary breakwater off Consumer Power Company's Palisades nuclear plant near South Haven in 1968, but it went to pieces during the winter of 1969-1970 and was scrapped.

The vessel was built as the *Sarnolite* in 1916 at Collingwood, and carried the name *Imperial Sarnia* in 1947 and 1948.

# Moonlight Crash

Crew members on the German freighter *Emsstein* were thanking their good fortune that they decided against their usual game of cards the night of October 6, 1966.

When the Liberian ship *Olympic Pearl* hit the side of the *Emsstein* at 9:10 PM the *Pearl's* bow broke through the steel plating and destroyed the officer's mess. It was the very spot where the men always played cards. "We were in our cabins drinking beer," one man grinned afterward.

Nobody could explain why the two ships collided that clear, moonlight night on the St. Clair River, just south of the town of St. Clair, Michigan. The *Pearl* hit the *Emsstein* on the port side, her projecting cutwater raking the *Emsstein's* hull and opening a hundred-foot gash below the water line before the upper bow drove deep into the side of the German's freighter's superstructure.

**Workers on the *Emsstein* were glad they weren't playing a usual game of cards the night it sank in a collision on the St. Clair River.**

Sparks from the crash ignited the *Emsstein's* cargo of chemicals causing a spectacular and dangerous blaze. Nobody was hurt.

The *Emsstein* drifted aground on the Canadian side of the river, where the stricken ship settled in the mud and took a steep list to port. Coast Guard vessels and private tugs removed the crew members and extinguished the fire.

The *Olympic Pearl* was not severely damaged, and was allowed to continue on down the river on its own power a few hours later.

The *Emsstein* was raised and towed to Detroit for repair fifteen days later. She never returned to the Great Lakes after that trip. The ship was scrapped in 1980.

# The *Fitzgerald* Mystery

The foundering of the ore carrier *Edmund Fitzgerald* on Lake Superior on November 10, 1975 remains the most celebrated shipwreck on the Great Lakes. Gordon Lightfoot's popular song about the wreck may have had something to do with stirring the legend. So did the fact that the *Fitzgerald* was the largest ship ever to sink on the lakes in modern times.

There is yet another reason for the popularity of the *Fitzgerald* story every autumn. The sinking generated a mystery. Nobody knows why the big freighter sank. Even the twenty-nine sailors who died with their ship probably didn't know.

Capt. Ernest "Mac" McSorley was talking by radio to Capt. Jesse Cooper, master of the nearby freighter *Arthur M. Anderson* just minutes before the lake swallowed the *Fitzgerald,* and he didn't indicate that anything was seriously wrong. "He told me had lost two vents and he said that he had a list . . . " Cooper told a board of inquiry. "He gave no indication that he was worried or that he had a problem or there was something that he couldn't cope with."

Cooper said he was shocked at the way that the *Fitzgerald* disappeared. He said it happened sometime after 7:10 PM after Morgan Clark, the *Anderson's* first mate, radioed positions to the *Fitzgerald.* They were temporarily blinded by a heavy snow squall in the area. The two vessels were only about eight miles apart and Cooper said the *Fitzgerald* was clearly visible on his radar screen. Then, without warning, the image on the screen disappeared. "The center of the scope was just a white blob." After ten or fifteen minutes the snow cleared and Cooper said "you could see for miles. We were looking for him. Everybody in the wheelhouse was looking for him. I called the *Fitzgerald* on the FM (radio) and I got no response."

Cooper said the U.S. Coast Guard station at Sault Ste. Marie was having radio trouble that night so he couldn't report the disappearance of the *Fitzgerald* until 7:50 PM, at least

The foundering of the *Edmund Fitzgerald* on Lake Superior in 1975 remains a mystery.

thirty minutes after it happened. "I informed them of my concern over the *Fitzgerald,* that I thought she had foundered. Then there was another ten or twelve minute lapse. I called them again. I think they were like I was. I don't think they could believe a ship could go down that fast."

It took the Coast Guard nearly two years to come up with a theory that defective hatch covers caused the sinking. That theory has been disputed by experienced lakes pilots who believe the *Fitzgerald* broke her spine on Lake Superior's notorious Caribou Shoal.

The theory that the *Fitzgerald* "shoaled out" may have started with Capt. Cooper but it was advanced in 1981 by author Robert J. Hemming in his book *Gales of November, The Sinking of the Edmund Fitzgerald.* The shoal, a long stretch of rock off Caribou Island that lies about twenty-six feet under the surface of Lake Superior, is believed to have snared more than one unwary ship. It is deep enough that it can't be seen by approaching vessels, and on a calm day, boats with a twenty-five-foot draft can pass right over it without any problem. During a gale, however, when the seas are rolling, any vessel caught on the down-side of a wave could drop down hard on Caribou Shoal, the pilots warn. Capt. Donald Erickson, who was in the same storm on Lake Superior on the freighter *William Clay Ford;* William S. LaParl, who served as senior second engineer aboard the *Fitzgerald* on her maiden trip, and Thomas Farnquist, director of the Great Lakes Shipwreck Historical Society in Sault Ste. Marie, all say they believe the *Fitzgerald* probably hit the shoal.

Farnquist said it was possible that the sailors aboard the *Fitzgerald* never realized the accident happened because of the way the ship was being buffeted by the storm. Erickson said the *Fitzgerald* passed Caribou Island and got very close to the shoal on its way toward Sault Ste. Marie. He said McSorley's own report to Cooper that the vessel was taking on water, was listing, and that two ballast tank vents were lost, were clues that something serious happened to the ship.

LaParl said the lost vent caps support the theory that the *Fitzgerald* hit bottom. "Those caps have a big threaded rod in the center. When you screw them down, a wave isn't ever going to knock them off. But if they stove in the bottom of the ship and built up enough internal pressure, it could have blown them off." LaParl said he knew most of the men on the *Fitzgerald* and was a close personal friend of George Holl, the chief engineer. "George and Capt. McSorley were both going to retire after that trip. It was going to be the last trip of their career. I guess it really was," LaParl said. "It was a sad thing. I can't help but think about those guys."

The ship lies in five hundred thirty feet of water, apparently with the bodies of the sailors still inside. Video footage of the wreck shot in 1989 through the Michigan Sea Grant Program indicates that the *Fitzgerald* hit the bottom bow first, then broke into two parts as it settled. The bow section is upright, while the stern section rests upside down at about a fifty-degree angle.

Sea Grant spokesman Kenneth Vrana said there is about a two hundred-foot-long gap between the two sections, with a lot of debris, including twenty-six thousand tons of taconite iron-ore pellets, the ship's cargo, piled in the middle. A lot of taconite is piled on top of the bow section, which means the *Fitzgerald* somehow dumped part of the load on top of itself when it hit bottom, Vrana said.

He said viewing the video film gave him "an eerie feeling."

# Glossery of Nautical Terms

Aft: The rear, or stern end of a ship.

Anchor: A heavy object attached to a ship by chain or cable, which, when thrown overboard, will hold the vessel in place.

Barge: A roomy, sometimes flat-bottomed ship designed to carry bulk cargo. It can move under sail, be towed, or be powered by an engine.

Bow: The front or forward part of a ship.

Bridge: A platform erected above and across the deck of a ship from where the vessel is operated.

Bulkhead: Any petition separating compartments of a ship.

Bulwark: The side of a ship above the upper deck.

Buoy: A floating marker anchored in water to show locations of channels or sunken obstacles.

Forecastle: The forward part of a ship where sailors live.

Founder: Sinking of a ship.

Galley: Kitchen of a ship.

Gangway: A door in the side or on a bulkhead of a ship.

Hatch: The covering of an opening on a ship's deck.

Hawser: A thick rope or cable used in pulling or anchoring or mooring a ship.

Hold: The interior of a ship below the lower deck where cargo is stowed.

Hook: Anchor.

Lifeboat: A small boat on a ship used to escape in case of trouble.

Lighter: A large, flat-bottomed boat or scow used to carry cargo to and from ships across shallow water to land.

Pilot: The person who steers a ship.

Pilothouse (or wheelhouse): The place on a ship where the pilot steers the vessel.

Propeller: A motorized vessel driven through the water by propellers.

Port: The left side of a ship to a person on the deck and looking forward toward the bow.

Porthole: An opening or window in the side of a ship.

Reef: A chain of rocks or earth lying near the surface of the water. Also used as a verb which means reducing the amount of working canvass on a sailing ship.

Rigging: The ropes and pulleys that support and control a ship's sails, masts and spars. Also a word used to describe the design of a ship.

Schooner: A sailing ship with fore and aft rigging.

Scow: A large flat-bottomed boat with broad, square ends.

Side-wheeler (or side-wheel steamer): A steam powered vessel propelled through the water by large paddle wheels mounted on both sides.

Starboard: The right side of a ship to a person on the deck and looking forward toward the bow.

Steamboat (or steamer, steamship): Any vessel powered by a steam engine. In old accounts, most commonly used for ships propelled by side-mounted paddle wheels.

Stern: The rear, or aft end of a ship.

Superstructure: The cabins, pilot house and other buildings erected above the main deck of a ship.

Tug (or tugboat): A ship with powerful engines designed for towing.

Waterlogged: The condition of a wooden ship in a sinking condition, but buoyed up by a cargo of material that is lighter than water.

Wharf: A dock or pier used in loading or unloading ships.

Yawl: A lifeboat on a ship.

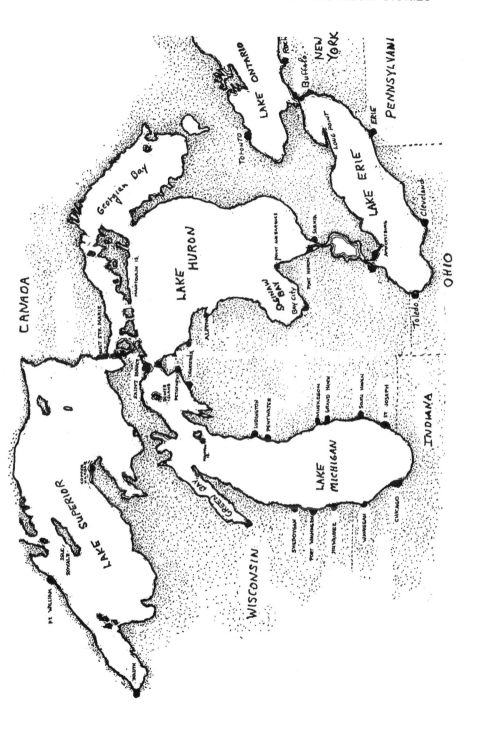

# About the Author

James L. Donahue was born June 1, 1938 at Harbor Beach, Michigan. He discovered an interest in writing in high school and took a part-time job on the *Harbor Beach Times.* While in college, Donahue took a year off from his studies to work for the *Huron Daily Tribune,* Bad Axe, Michigan. Following graduation from Central Michigan University with majors in Journalism and English literature, Donahue went to work for the former *News-Palladium* in Benton Harbor, Michigan, worked two years at the *Kalamazoo Gazette,* Kalamazoo, Michigan, and finally became Sanilac County bureau chief for the *Times Herald,* Port Huron, Michigan, in 1971. He retired in 1993 to found Anchor Publications, a family-owned publishing business involved in literary and historical writing and research.

Donahue writes a syndicated weekly column for the Times *Herald,* the *Mining Journal,* Marquette, Mich., and the *Huron Daily Tribune,* Bad Axe, Mich., about shipwrecks and other historical events on the lakes. His stories also have appeared in the *Grand Rapids Press* and the *Traverse City Record Eagle.* In 1991, Donahue included seventy-five of his best stories in a collection titled *Terrifying Steamboat Stories,* published by Altwerger & Mandel Publishing Co.

Among his most recent books is *Schooners in Peril,* a collection of stories about sailing ships on the lakes and the terrible things that happened to them.

Donahue collaborated with Judge James H. Lincoln, Harbor Beach, Michigan, in the book *Fiery Trial,* a historical account of a forest fire that swept the Thumb Area of Michigan in 1881. *Fiery Trial* was published by the Historical Society of Michigan in 1984. Anchor Publications reprinted a revised form of *Fiery Trial,* with the cooperation of the Historical Society, in 1994. In 1982, Donahue and his wife, Doris, owned and used an old-time wood-burning cook stove in their home. They wrote and published *Cooking On Iron*, a collection of early American recipes ranging from Chestnut Soup and Hickory Nut Cake, to making soap. His story, *The Day We Wrecked the Train*, a personal account about growing up in Harbor Beach, appeared in a special edition of *Good Old Days Magazine* in 1987.

Donahue also wrote and published *Steaming Through Smoke and Fire 1871* and *Steamboats in Ice 1872*. The books are a collection of true stories about shipwrecks and other events affecting vessels on the Great Lakes during the years 1871 and 1872.

James and Doris Donahue live near Cass City, Mich., with their daughter, Jennifer. The Donahues have three other children; Aaron, who lives with his wife, Gayle, in California, Ayn Bishop, of Georgia, and Susie Donahue, who lives in Germany.

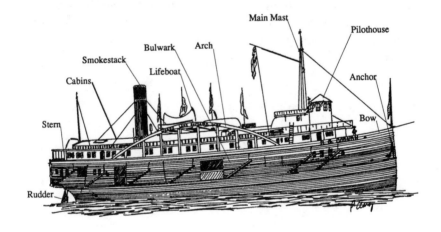